SILENT CRY

A NOVEL

DR. JESSICA THOMPSON

Ballast Books, LLC
www.ballastbooks.com

Copyright © 2024 by Jessica Thompson

All rights reserved. No part of this book may be reproduced in any form or by any electronic or mechanical means, including information storage and retrieval systems, without permission in writing from the publisher, except by reviewers, who may quote brief passages in a review.

ISBN: 978-1-962202-43-5

Printed in Hong Kong

Published by Ballast Books
www.ballastbooks.com

For more information, bulk orders, appearances, or speaking requests,
please email: info@ballastbooks.com

*To my husband in honor of all the craziness
we encountered throughout our careers.
You can't make this stuff up!*

CHAPTER

1

Late night in a small town. Kate was wiping down the coffee counter at the café. It was almost time for her shift to end. Intent upon her task, she finished arranging the coffee cups for the opening crew in the morning and made sure all the coffee flavors were full to the brim. After looking over her work, she reached for her purse and bag under the counter and turned off the lights.

He knew exactly when she got off work. He would often sit in his car across the street just watching her through the café's windows. It was not unusual for him to sit there. He loved watching the cars go up and down the road. As people passed, he would wave. Eventually, he became a permanent figure in the parking lot.

God, she was gorgeous. Tall with dark hair that flowed over her shoulders. She had a way about her, sort of mischievous yet sexy. She knew how to look alluring but not cheap. She respected herself in that way at least. He was lucky that she found him interesting since he was older than her.

Kate was special. Special because she had a hidden secret that only he knew about. That's how their relationship had started—because he'd discovered her secret. Maybe he used it as blackmail, or maybe she was actually interested in him. It didn't matter because, tonight, he was ending the relationship.

You see, Kate had a problem. That was her secret. He'd run across her one day down by the river. It was a remote part of town, but younger kids would go down to that area in the summer to swim. This time of year, there wasn't much traffic down there. He would occasionally drive by just to clear his head and make sure everything was on the up-and-up.

That's where he'd found Kate all alone. She was settled on a large, flat rock that kids would jump off. She sat there crossed-legged with her arms resting on her knees, apparently in a state of meditation—or at least that's what he thought. He stared at her through his side window for a few minutes before he opened his car door and approached her.

At first, he wasn't even sure who was sitting by the riverbank. However, as he got closer, he realized it was Kate—but something wasn't right. She was a weird pale gray color. Some would say death warmed over. She turned her head in his direction when she heard him approach but didn't seem to have the energy to move. Listless and dull, Kate stared right at him, but it was more like she stared right through him.

That's when he realized her secret. He glanced across her body. On Kate's right arm was a tourniquet and a needle. He let out a sigh. Kate was high. It definitely wasn't the first time he'd seen someone high, but it was the first time he had seen Kate in this state. She sighed and let her head droop forward. She was so high, the rest of her body followed. Her dark brown hair fell, covering her beautiful face as she doubled over, almost folding into herself.

He stood there for a bit, contemplating the situation and how he should proceed. Finally, he slowly sat down beside her.

It was like sneaking up on an injured animal. You don't want to spook it for fear it will hurt itself.

Although Kate saw him taking a seat beside her, she definitely wasn't processing it. Taking a measured pace, he deliberately leaned around her and removed the needle and tourniquet from her arm. There were drugs still left in the syringe. At least she hadn't used it all at once; otherwise, he would have found her in a different state altogether.

As he sat there, he decided to let her come out of it, no matter how long it took. He put his arm around her and drew her next to his warm body; the temperature this time of year could still be quite chilly. Then, he continually checked his watch every few minutes to keep some sense of the time. They sat there in silence for over an hour. As the time went by, he took the opportunity to really take a good look at her. He studied her face as she leaned her head on his shoulder. In his opinion, she was quite beautiful. He had never taken the time to just look at her, but now that he could spend as much time as he wanted examining her features, he couldn't deny her striking appearance.

Sure, he had known of Kate before this, but just in passing. After all, Seneca Rocks was a small town. If you didn't know someone, gossip soon prevailed. Kate was young, early twenties. She'd come from a good home and could've had the world, but she didn't want to leave Seneca Rocks. Unfortunately, there wasn't much around here for employment other than the typical mom-and-pop joints. She lucked into a full-time job at the café when it opened. The owner really liked her, so she used it as her reason to stay. Plus, she was a good worker. She would take on extra shifts, usually closing the place down.

He could feel her shiver every once in a while. She wasn't dressed for these temperatures, especially down by the river. The cold wind seemed even colder as it blew across the barely moving water. He listened to the crackle of the stream and the rustling of the wind through the bare branches. It was almost deafeningly quiet except for the stream. Birds hadn't yet returned to the area from their southern habitats.

He loved being outdoors. It was where he felt the most at peace with the world. No wonder Kate chose this spot. The tranquility of the scene gave one the opportunity to reflect on life. It remained charmingly serene despite the presence of someone being ravaged by drugs.

Kate suddenly turned her head to him, still silent, and started to cry. She registered who he was and feared the worst. He just put his arms around her in a big bear hug and let her cry it out. He wasn't sure how long they sat there in this reassuring embrace. Eventually, her tears were replaced with the sound of the creek and the wind blowing through the trees.

Carefully, he helped Kate up from the riverbank and guided her back to his car. The process was slow, as she was unsteady on her feet. For as little as she weighed, she felt like a ton as he was trying to steer her in the right direction. He assumed she had walked to the swimming hole from the café. It wasn't that far, and he didn't see another car around. And after all, walking into remote areas would make it easier for her to hide her secret.

He opened up the passenger side car door, and she slid in. Since she was unable to do much herself, he grasped the seatbelt and strapped her in. When he closed the passenger door, she looked at him through the window with a concerned face and continued to watch him as he rounded the front of the car. As he slipped behind the wheel, Kate slowly became anxious about the reality of the situation and started fidgeting in her seat. She began running her hands along the door, getting a feel for the lock and handle like she was blind. Glancing shrewdly at her, he thought she may open the door and make a break for it.

"What's going to happen to me?" she asked as she clasped her hands together and put them between her knees.

"Well, you're lucky I found you when I did. Today could have had a very different ending." He glanced at her as he put the car into drive. She was silently shaking her head, her beautiful brown hair slowing swinging back and forth with the movement of her head. "What would you like to happen?" he countered.

"Can we keep it our secret?" And that's how it started. Her secret became his.

He remembered nodding his head in answer, a brief smile crossing her lips as he turned away from her. Before long, he pulled into the café's parking lot. For a while, they sat in his car in silence. He didn't want to rush her as her senses started to return. The town seemed calmer in the evenings, and today was no different. At last, she reached for the handle and opened the door. He watched her as she made her way to her car parked on the far side of the lot.

Once she was safely in her vehicle, he glanced down and stared at the drug paraphernalia on the floorboard while contemplating how to get rid of her evidence. Moments later, he heard her car start up as she backed out of the parking lot and pulled onto the main road in the direction of her parents' house. Wanting to make sure she made it home, he slowly eased his car out behind her. Once she pulled into the driveway, she stuck her hand out the window and waved as he passed by. A slow smile crept across his face as he headed to his destination.

The secret they shared had developed into more. Although he'd just discovered her secret a little over a month before, their relationship had progressed into a romantic one. At the beginning, he would visit her every day at the café, ordering his usual mocha latte. Laidback as ever, he would sit at the bar, decompressing after work. Although they didn't share many words, he kept his eye on her. Community members would amble in and out, carrying on casual conversation with him as they passed. All the while, the tension between him and Kate increased. In time, he and Kate became a couple—in secret, of course.

On this night, Kate walked out of the café at exactly eleven o'clock. He watched while she turned off the open sign as she walked out of the café's door. She turned and put her key in the lock, making sure all was secure. Then, he saw her glance over at him and smile. She wore tight jeans and a sweatshirt that proudly advertised the café with her hair pulled back into a ponytail.

Kate sauntered over to his car, her shoes crunching on the gravel as she crossed the parking lot. When she reached the vehicle, she threw her bags in the back and got in the passenger seat. This was the typical routine when she got off work. They would spend a couple of hours together every night, and then he would drop her back off at the café so she could pick up her vehicle. Most evenings, they would go for a walk down by the river since it had meaning for both of them. It was easier to take one vehicle—and less noticeable too.

Today, however, Kate hadn't driven to the café. She was planning on going on a vacation—or, at least, that's what she'd told her boss and her family. Her parents thought that she and a few friends were heading to the beach and that they were going to pick her up after her shift was over to head out of town. Actually, he and Kate had planned a weekend getaway, just the two of them. Or that's what she thought.

Kate was so excited for this weekend. He'd told her exactly how to arrange it so that it looked like she was heading out for a weekend vacation with her girlfriends. The whole thing was a little funny if she thought about it because Kate really didn't have many friends. At least, not the kind that she hung out with. She had more acquaintances really. Those she depended on for her secret. Nonetheless, this was the cover story, and her lie had gone undetected so far.

She had no idea what was in store for her.

CHAPTER
2

The first day of spring and the following couple of months in West Virginia can sometimes be temperamental, making it tricky when one is attempting to dress for the day. The mornings can be quite frigid with a dense fog that takes its time to clear, but by early afternoon, you may be sweating your ass off. Not to mention there may be a freak snowstorm or hailstorm somewhere in between. Dressing in layers is typically the way to go.

Raelynn took all of this into consideration as she stood in her skivvies, pondering her attire in her closet. It usually wasn't too difficult for her to pick her outfit for the day, as her uniform typically consisted of khakis and a dress shirt. She tried to keep her wardrobe minimal because if she had to put on the bulletproof vest, layers could make it impossible to move. The heavy weight of the vest felt like a boa constrictor, slowly squeezing, taking her last breath.

Although the last time she'd been concerned enough to don her lovely vest was when old Mr. Mercer had been on the roof of his barn with a rifle, cranking out rounds at invisible people who kept "stealing his gasoline out of his tractor." It had taken three hours to convince him to get down on this occasion. Unfortunately, this was a call she got every few weeks since Mr. Mercer had early onset Alzheimer's, and passersby never knew when he might mistake them for a gas thief.

With a disgusted sigh, Raelynn grabbed a red button-down shirt, tucked her tails into her khakis, and slipped her feet in her favorite Sperrys. Maybe she'd change it up when it got warmer, but right now, she wasn't going to put too much thought into it. She hadn't changed anything about herself since joining the police force right after graduation from college. It was hard to imagine that had been almost twenty years ago. Forty was creeping up quick. The only thing that had changed for Raelynn was that she'd advanced through the department rather quickly—although it wasn't too hard since the department only had ten officers, including the chief. Raelynn had endured the rank of patrolman for ten years before being promoted to sergeant. Then, a few months after, she'd been chosen to be the only detective in the department. The pay wasn't great, but it put food on the table. Besides, the inheritance left to her by her parents was a nice supplement.

Raelynn definitely wouldn't complain about being the only detective, especially since Seneca Rocks wasn't considered a major metropolitan area. When a major crime happened, it was what everyone talked about for a long time, which could be considered good and bad. The last major event had been when the local butcher and his wife got divorced. He'd gone on a major bender, which had led to him using an electric cattle prod on his wife's new fling. Needless to say, the new fling received second-degree burns on a place that made it hard to sit down for quite a while, and the butcher got an unlawful assault charge, which led to him spending two weeks in the county jail. Yep, major drama around here.

After a quick glance in the mirror, Raelynn pulled her auburn hair into her everyday ponytail, strapped on her badge and gun, grabbed a light jacket, and stepped out into the brisk breeze of an April morning. Although it was slightly on the chilly side today, the sky was blue, and the sun was shining. The forecast proclaimed it was going to be seventy-five degrees by the end of the day. Summer was just around the corner.

Nevertheless, Raelynn shivered as she locked her front door and strode over to her standard-issue black Ford Explorer. There was a thin covering of dew on the windows. She jumped in the driver's seat and started her cruiser. Reaching over, she turned on the heater and hit the windshield wipers to clear her view. The police radio instantly came to life, and she radioed dispatch that she was currently on duty and available for calls.

Raelynn had always been interested in crime and had known that she wanted to be a police officer since she was little. She especially loved being a detective and had been training for this position for the past fifteen years, even before she got hired into the police department. While in high school and college, she'd jumped on any chance to gain information. She would attend camps in the summertime and go to any special lectures within driving distance. Plus, once she'd been officially hired in the police department, she'd been sure to attend any special investigative training she could find, even though she knew she probably wouldn't use much of it while at her department. She didn't like to toot her own horn, but she was the only college graduate in the department. Although she believed there was nothing wrong with not attending college, she admitted it did give her a leg up in certain situations.

The drive from her house into town took about ten minutes. All roads leading into Seneca Rocks consisted of two-lane highways containing potholes of various sizes, some so large you could lose your vehicle if you hit it just right. The winter months in this part of West Virginia wreaked havoc on the roadways. Deep snows with constant plowing and ice melt ate the roadways away. Though spring was approaching, it was still too early for the local department of highways to begin paving the roads, as there could always be a late snow squall that hit the area.

Raelynn stopped at the local coffee shop to grab a quick cup of joe. There wasn't a whole lot of selection for beverage services and restaurants in Seneca Rocks. There definitely weren't name brand eateries, just basic hole-in-the-wall mom-and-pop places. The café was an attempt to bring Seneca Rocks into a new age.

Raelynn had to admit the owner had done a pretty good job. The café had a homey feeling yet provided an atmosphere that made patrons feel alive. There was modern music every weekend but not the head-banging type. During the summer months, the bands would be set up outside, which brought even more customers than usual. Inside, the seating was casual yet comfy. Booths and tables filled most of the open area. The café was housed in a rehabbed feed and grain store. The wide oak plank floors were the originals, along with the counter area. A new coat of paint had been applied to the walls, and copper tin had been added to the ceiling. This resulted in a fresh look that was appealing to customers looking for a relaxed setting in which to hang out.

The usual patrons were sitting at their table, enjoying a newspaper and town gossip. This group included the mayor, a retired farmer, and a gentleman from the bank. A bus driver, recently finished with his route, made up the foursome.

Raelynn glanced over, and they all exchanged a casual wave. After paying for her special cup of joe, which happened to be a caramel latte, Raelynn jumped back into her cruiser and headed to her home away from home, the Seneca Rocks Police Department.

Raelynn had worked all different shifts while on patrol. She happily confessed that being a detective assigned to day shift had improved her attitude, but that was really the only thing in her life that had improved. It was true that switching to working days had increased her availability to go on dates, but Raelynn just hadn't found someone who interested her. Actually, she couldn't even remember the last time she'd gone on a date. She enjoyed spending time with her friend, a nurse at the hospital, but they rarely got together anymore either. Most of the time, Raelynn simply relaxed at home on her porch with her favorite drink.

Raelynn pulled her cruiser into her designated spot in front of the police station. They didn't have assigned spaces, but everyone knew where one another parked. If your space wasn't available, it instantly sparked an inquisition before you entered the police station.

The police department Raelynn called home had a . . . somewhat intriguing origin story. It was rumored that once the Prohibition ended, the state police couldn't quite handle the increase in crime in the county. Pendleton County was quite large in terms of geographical area, and response time for crime was deemed to be lacking. After all, the state police were only equipped with three troopers for the entire county. Although the population never grew to more than ten thousand people, there seemed to be enough justification to add additional officers. Therefore, Seneca Rocks Police was incorporated.

The Seneca Rocks Police Department had been housed in the same building since its inception in the early 1940s. As the department grew in officers, additional space was erected onto the building. Currently, the Seneca Rocks Police Department consisted of the chief, one detective, and eight officers that covered calls 24-7. The department also had an overnight holding cell, typically used for those arrested for driving under the influence. The department was a typical concrete structure painted a light gray that got touched up whenever a local citizen was condemned to community service hours. The only identifiable sign was the department's badge that had been painted onto the glass entrance doors.

Raelynn knew it wasn't going to be a good day as she pushed the entry door open. There were too many officers in the office. A typical day consisted of Chief Austin, herself, and two patrolmen, usually the same two every shift: Dane and Tony. The evening and night shift consisted of a sergeant and two more patrolmen. Today, it seemed like everyone was here.

As Raelynn crossed the squad room to her office, she could see Chief Austin on the telephone, and he didn't look happy. Just as she rounded the corner of her desk, she heard the chief's loud voice boom across the room.

"Raelynn, get in here."

Chief Anthony Austin had the demeanor of a drill sergeant when running the department, but he really was a compassionate guy when it came to family and friends. He was one of those individuals who didn't want his department to look bad and kept everyone on their toes. Raelynn had learned a lot from the chief over the years and thought of him as her mentor.

In addition, Chief Austin had a military background. He'd been deployed as a Marine in the Vietnam War in the 1970s, so it was understandable why he would run a tight ship. After Vietnam, he'd returned home, joined the police force, and married his high school sweetheart, Carrie. Back then, the police department had comprised four people, so it hadn't taken Chief Austin long to rise through the ranks and become chief. Over the years, he and Carrie's family had grown by two twin boys, both in college now. Carrie was the town's librarian and hosted a monthly book club, which Raelynn had attended a time or two.

Raelynn didn't even set down her unfinished cup of coffee. Instead, she did a 180 and walked to the chief's office.

Chief Austin was a macho man by first appearance, coming in at six foot three and weighing every bit of 250 pounds. He'd stayed fit through the years and typically carried himself with great stature. Today, though, was not one of those days. Raelynn had never seen the chief look so wilted. He looked like one of those three-day-old helium balloons that was leaking air and only floating about three feet off the ground. Yep, just deflated. As Raelynn rounded the doorframe, Chief Austin's face stopped her dead in her tracks.

"We've got a body." Chief Austin motioned for Raelynn to take a seat across from him. "A hunter found the body of a female on the Allegheny Mountain Trail. I don't have a lot of information yet. The hunter is from out of town and had to walk about two miles back into town to make the call to us. He sounded pretty shaken up on the phone. I sent Monte to meet him at the diner so he can take him back up to the body and secure the scene."

That would explain why she hadn't seen Monte in the office when she'd arrived. Monte Anderson was a veteran of the police department and a descendant of the Cherokee tribe that had settled in the Seneca Rocks area. He knew all the mountains and valleys in this region like the back of his hand. So it made sense for Monte to go back into the woods with the hunter.

The news that Raelynn had just been presented left her dumbfounded. However, she realized that Chief Austin was still talking to her and tried to concentrate on what he was saying.

"I called the whole team in for this. We probably won't need everyone, but I wanted us to be covered. They are packing up the crime scene equipment and loading up. I don't want to draw a lot of attention to this yet—not until we get a better picture of who it is and what may be going on." His worried face became more serious than ever. "Obviously, I want you as the lead on this, Raelynn. We are going to treat this as a homicide until we can determine otherwise. Pick a few officers you want to take with you to handle the scene. The rest will be here for support. I called the county coroner. She should be here within the hour to go with you."

This was the first potential homicide since her promotion to detective. Sure, she had seen her share of dead bodies, but it was usually those who had died of natural causes or a random vehicle accident. *This*—this was different. Raelynn could feel her body become high with anxiety over the news. Her adrenaline was beginning to kick in with full effect.

Ready to get moving, Raelynn downed the last of her coffee, tossed the cup in the chief's garbage can, and stood up to leave. Before exiting the chief's office, she turned back and stated in a determined tone, "Don't worry, Chief. We'll figure this out."

He just looked at her with a somber face and shook his head before dismissing her with a wave of his hand.

As Raelynn approached the door to the squad room, mentally analyzing the officers left for her to choose from, Chief Austin mentioned one last thing. "Oh, Raelynn? Try not to get too emotional after getting up there. I'm 99 percent sure we're going to be able to identify her right away. Not too many people we don't know around here."

Raelynn nodded as she stepped into the chaos of those packing equipment for the ride. She had never seen so many officers moving so quickly. After swiftly evaluating the situation, she opted to take two of them—Dane and Tony—with her to the crime scene. They weren't at the same level as Monte, but he would already be there anyway. And Dane and Tony were pretty sharp, with a keen eye for detail. Raelynn felt confident they could contribute something to the investigation by helping at the scene itself.

To be fair, she hadn't been overly impressed by Dane at the beginning. When he was a new recruit who had just graduated from the police academy, he had loudly praised himself for being the DUI expert. Of course, it wasn't hard to become an expert when you worked the weekend evening shift and kept catching the same crew coming from the Rowdy Rascal bar the next town over. Raelynn would have thought the crew would figure out an officer sat in the same exact spot every Friday night, or maybe they just liked giving the new guy a hard time. Either way, they sure knew how to press Dane's buttons. They typically carpooled and traded places in the vehicle before he got up to them. Then, they'd all deny who was driving, so Dane would just take them all home and give them a stern lecture on drinking and driving. An expert indeed.

Despite his less than impressive start, Dane eventually eased up on his cockiness and began focusing on what mattered most: the community. Although he initially cared about his reputation and how he looked to others, he grew to demonstrate a strong devotion to Seneca Rocks and the safety and welfare of those who lived there alongside him. He could still be a bit of a clown sometimes, but he knew how to be serious when it counted—and now was that time.

Tony had always been quite different from Dane. A bit more shy and reserved, he hadn't stuck out to Raelynn at first because he seemed to slink in the shadows. However, he really showcased his passion for the job when he went on a high-speed chase after a man who had assaulted his girlfriend and tried to escape in his beat-up Corolla. Tony had stayed in pursuit, even after the man had stuck a firearm out the window, shouting that he would shoot anyone who tried to stop him from getting away. Fortunately, the raving man had blown a tire shortly thereafter, and despite his loud mouth, he'd been detained by Tony with fairly minimal resistance.

That didn't diminish Raelynn's pride in him though. Tony hadn't backed down, hadn't been intimidated, and hadn't hesitated when the moment came to get that domestic abuser off the streets. Tony had recognized the man's volatility and understood that he could hurt innocent bystanders with his gun. Without worrying about his own safety, he had done what needed to be done to hold the perpetrator accountable and protect his town.

Needless to say, Raelynn was pretty satisfied with her selection of officers to accompany her to the "crime scene"—if a crime had even occurred. Those whom she decided should stay—Jamie and Elissa—were the ones who had more social skills and could more effectively retrieve or deliver information. A time like this required an officer that showed empathy, especially when talking to the victim's family. Plus, the officers coming off of night shift would be no use to her in the field. She wanted someone who'd had a good night's sleep and maintained a clear head. With that in mind, she made a mental note to not keep Monte out too long either. He was the sergeant on night shift, and she didn't want him too exhausted before his next shift.

Just as Raelynn finished instructing the rest of the officers to load the equipment into two squad cars, the front door of the police department opened to reveal the Seneca Rocks coroner. Darla Anderson, the county coroner and also Monte's wife, was still dressed in her nursing scrubs. She had been in the middle of a twelve-hour shift at the local hospital's emergency room when the chief had called.

It wasn't surprising that Darla had taken this side gig when the former coroner had passed away. Since marrying Monte five years previously, Darla had developed firsthand knowledge of what it was like living with a police officer and caring for both victims and suspects in the emergency room. Besides, the whole coroner thing definitely couldn't pay the bills, but the hospital worked great to donate her services to the county.

After approaching with her typical warm smile (somewhat tighter than usual given the circumstances), Darla leaned in and gave Raelynn a hug. They had been friends since high school, and in fact, Raelynn was the one who had introduced Darla to Monte. Sometimes, Raelynn was struck by how ironic it was that she could fix other people's relationship problems but couldn't resolve her own.

Moments later, the women jumped into the front seats of Raelynn's Explorer while the assisting officers climbed into two other patrol cars. They were on their way to what was being treated as a crime scene.

Monte had radioed the location as the Seneca Creek trailhead, which didn't come as a surprise for Raelynn. The park service did a fantastic job of maintaining the various trails throughout the county, and this trail was probably the most visited in the area. Seneca Rocks was a prime tourist vacation spot, especially for rock climbing and hiking in the summer months. This trail was particularly popular because it had multiple waterfalls and shallow pools used for swimming. Hunters also used these trails throughout the year, and spring gobbler season had just taken off.

Unfortunately, the group didn't have any additional information from Monte about the crime scene. The chief had instructed them to limit radio traffic because everyone seemed to have a scanner in their home, and he didn't want to cause panic in the community if someone overheard the officers swapping information.

It was impossible for them to know what they were getting themselves into. Raelynn's first thought was that they could just have an accidental shooting on their hands, it being turkey season and all. It was amazing how many hunters would mistake other people for wild game.

A few years ago, two brothers had been out squirrel hunting when one ended up shooting the other. Thankfully, the brother was a bad shot and just got him in the leg. However, Raelynn had heard he screamed and cried like a girl. After a night in the hospital with a short surgery to remove the pellets, the injured hunter was able to go home. His brother was in tears the entire time and never left his side. The prosecuting attorney said the pain of shooting your brother was enough punishment and chose not to press charges. Now, they both could laugh about it, but the situation wasn't brought up very often.

On the other hand, there weren't a whole lot of females engaged in hunting around these parts. Most participated in recreational shooting either at the range or in an open field. For those who did hunt, they were typically escorted by their male counterparts and used as spotters, who remained near the shooter's side at all times. So the likelihood that it was an accidental shooting seemed slim.

On the drive out, Raelynn mentally consulted all of her training to organize her thought processes once they got on scene. Only time would tell the truth of what had happened. They would know soon enough.

CHAPTER
3

Living in a small town like Seneca Rocks was tough. To the general public, it looked like the perfect place to live. Everyone knew everyone, but that was the first problem. If you came from a good family—and the whole town was essentially composed of good families—then you were expected to live up to high standards. That was the second problem.

Kate's secret had started in high school. At that time, she was the all-American girl. She got good grades in school, was a cheerleader, and had a great personality. People didn't realize the stress levels that came with all of that. The town had set the bar high. When you can't meet that standard, disappointment hits hard.

Kate's life had been going pretty well. At the time, she was dating the quarterback of the football team. Again, it was the type of relationship that was expected—the cheerleader and the football star.

Adam was tall and handsome with blond hair that fell casually into his blue eyes. He would often wear tank tops to show off his impressive muscles. For a teenager, Kate thought her dreams had come true. She envisioned her future with Adam: going to college, getting married, and starting a family. There was no doubt in her mind that she had found her true love.

Adam had come from a good home too. He wanted to go into business at the university. Adam was a hard worker. On the weekends and after football season, Adam helped out on farms around the county. Mainly, he was there for strength and labor, and he was always busy during hay season.

But everything changed for Kate one night. That evening, Adam was on his way home from an away football game. Usually, Kate would have been with him, but on this occasion, things turned out differently from how she'd planned.

In fact, she and Adam were in a bit of a fight. She couldn't even remember what the argument was about—probably something silly and irrelevant, like the fact that he hadn't called her before he'd left his house or that he'd seen her talking to another guy and didn't like it. After all, jealousy is a cruel tool; it makes you create scenarios in your mind that couldn't possibly happen. It's like the game telephone. You start by telling one person a sentence, and by the time it reaches the end of the line, it has been twisted into a completely different tale. That was much of her relationship with Adam.

Anyway, Adam and Kate fought so often at that point that it was a natural occurrence in their relationship. And it wasn't just yelling at each other. There had been times when Kate had lashed out physically. This only happened on a few occasions, but Adam bore the punishment. She'd been known to scratch viciously at his back as he was walking away from the argument or to run her hands through his hair and pull with all her might. There was something satisfying about physically transferring her emotional pain and frustration to him in that way.

Aside from the reason behind their fight, Kate remembered the night in vivid detail. The Seneca Rocks Indians, an appropriate mascot, had beaten one of the most difficult competitors in the state. Away trips involved being pretty far away from Seneca Rocks because the

Indians were only considered a division three school due to the lack of students Kate's parents had traveled to the game and met up with friends they'd gone to college with. Although they insisted that Kate go out with them after the game for a celebratory pizza, she simply didn't want to go with her parents. She had promised Adam she would ride back with him to work through whatever they'd been arguing about. Unfortunately, her parents refused to take no for an answer.

With heartbreaking clarity, Kate recalled Adam leaving and giving her a backward wave as he marched toward his car. Sullen and frustrated, she sat eating pizza with her family and their friends but wasn't mentally checked into the conversation. As a typical teenager, she didn't want to be there—she wanted to be with her boyfriend—so any participation from her was minimal.

It was close to eleven o'clock when the family car finally pulled into the driveway. Kate was exhausted, but she needed to call Adam. So she marched into the kitchen and grabbed the cordless phone. No cell phones in Seneca Rocks—the area was much too rural for getting a cell signal. She realized that she was calling late and Adam's parents would probably be annoyed, but she needed to tell him it wasn't her fault—she hadn't had a choice but to stay with her parents. But she knew Adam would be mad because she hadn't put him first.

When Kate rang Adams's house, the voicemail picked up. Disappointed, she listened as Adam's mom politely instructed the caller to please leave a message. Kate didn't. She wanted to but figured she would just deal with it in the morning. She was exhausted and wanted to curl up in her bed under the warmth of her down comforter.

Not long after dawn, Kate woke to her mom shaking her. Still sleep deprived, Kate tried getting the moth balls out of her head. Eventually, it struck her that her mom looked distraught. Why was she rousing her so early? It was a Saturday, and Kate preferred sleeping in late on the weekends, especially when there had been a football game the night before. She looked out the window and saw the sun just beginning to rise. It had to be early—too early for a wakeup call like this.

Through the fading film of sleep, Kate blinked at her mom but still couldn't process what was going on. Meanwhile, her mom was pacing the floor and growing more emotional as the minutes ticked by. Once Kate indicated she was at least semi-responsive, her mom sat on the edge of the bed and grabbed her hand. Kate remembered that soft touch, her mother's trembling fingers gently cupping Kate's. In that moment, she glanced down and noticed her mother's wedding ring, a single gold band. Nothing fancy—just acknowledgment of the bond. Kate let her eyes trail up to her mom's face. She was startled to see tears were ready to flow from her glistening eyes.

"Kate, there's been an accident," her mom quietly stated. Maybe it was the pause after the news, or maybe Kate's mom was just trying to deliver the message in snapshots so Kate could process them, but Kate's mind instantly jumped to her dad. He hadn't been in the best of health lately. Mom always said he didn't watch what he ate, although he would flatly deny the accusations of sneaking into the freezer for a late-night ice cream snack. Of course, his staunch denials were always paired with a slight smirk on his face and usually a wink at Kate.

"What happened? Is Dad okay?" Kate sat up straighter in her bed, pulling her comforter around her as protection.

"Dad's fine. It's Adam," her mom replied. There was another pause that felt denser than the last. As the seconds passed by with no further explanation, panic and anxiety began to swell in Kate's stomach. Her chest started to grow heavy, and she felt like a guppy outside of the fishbowl, gasping for air. Kate glanced at her mom with wide eyes and noticed the tears running down her cheeks. Taking no action to wipe them away, her mom kept her eyes locked on Kate's. Unaware

of her own actions, Kate began to rock back and forth, waiting for more information, suddenly completely alert when all she wanted at this point was for it to be a dream.

"Adam's parents just called. He didn't make it home last night. They said they saw you had called, but they were out looking for him and couldn't find him. I guess one of the officers from the Seneca Rocks Police Department found his car early this morning. They think he maybe fell asleep and veered off the road into a tree. From what they can tell, he was ejected from the car through the front window. They don't think he was wearing his seatbelt." With that pronouncement, Kate's mom burst into full-blown sobs. Having never seen her mother cry like this, Kate sat in stunned silence while her mom tried to regain her composure. The anxiety had quickly passed; now, numbness had set in. She took a deep breath and felt her lower lip start to tremble.

"Adam's gone," Kate stated. It wasn't really a question; it was more of an acknowledgment.

Her mom could only nod her head. Then, she reached out and pulled Kate into a big bear hug. As Kate laid her head on her mom's shoulder, she felt hot moisture streaking down her face. She hadn't even gotten to say goodbye to him. As she melted against her mom, feeling the warmth of her body and the solid protection of her arms wrapped around her, Kate was struck with a horrific realization. This was all her parents' fault.

"You made me stay and not go home with him." Abruptly lifting her head, Kate gazed straight at her mother with a hard expression. "It's your fault that Adam is dead. If you would have let me ride home with him, this would never have happened."

Kate's mom tilted her head slightly in shock. Her tears momentarily halted in response to the harsh words that had just been hurled at her. This reaction was to be expected, especially with teenagers. Kate hadn't gotten her way the night before, and now she needed someone to blame. The obvious choice would be her parents. Trying to keep that in mind and shove down any guilt rising up in her throat, Kate's mom slowly got up from the bed and walked to the bedroom door.

"Kate, you need some time to adjust to the news. Don't say anything else that you'll regret later. I'll come and check on you in a little bit." With that, her mom left, pulling the door gently shut behind her. The soft snap of the door closing caused Kate to jump, bringing her out of her blank state of mind. But she wasn't ready to face reality. She lay back down and pulled her comforter, her protection, around her as the tears began again.

Kate considered that to be the worst day of her life. She refused to come out of her room for a week. In fact, she didn't take a shower and barely touched the food her mom brought to her room. Attempting to be patient and understanding, her parents didn't push the issue with her until the day of the funeral. Kate had no intention of going. She had dropped into such a state of depression that she didn't care about anything. She had no interest in seeing Adam in a casket. She wanted to remember him alive and happy. However, she was haunted by the memory of him walking away and waving back at her. Maybe she deserved that. Maybe that was a signal to her that that was going to be the last time she would see him. All the maybes made her feel like she was going nuts.

On the day of the funeral, Kate's mom came to her room. After decisively opening the curtains, she stood at the bottom of Kate's bed. She'd had enough of how Kate was reacting.

"Time to get out of bed, Kate," her mom said in a stern voice, her hands on her hips. Kate didn't even acknowledge that she was there, keeping her whole body covered by her purple comforter.

Kate's mom was a respectable woman. She rarely revealed her emotional side, and Kate knew Adam's death had hit her hard. She'd really liked him. Kate assumed her mother was tired of her acting like a selfish child and not acknowledging Adam's death. Deep down, Kate understood that her mother's intentions were good, but mentally, she wasn't ready to face the world.

"Kate, you're going to this funeral. You need to make an appearance," her mother announced. A moment later, Kate felt the pull of the comforter. She let her mom take it from her without betraying any reaction. Finally, she slowly turned her head to look at her mom.

"Get up and take a shower. God knows you need one. I'll have breakfast ready for you when you get out."

Without looking up, Kate could hear her mom rummaging through her closet. It was probably for the best that her mom picked out her outfit. Ever so slowly, Kate faced the reality that she was gonna have to go to the funeral. She was going to have to look at people and see Adam. As her previously frozen brain ground back to life, Kate wondered if people would blame her for Adam's accident. But she kept telling herself that it wasn't her fault—it was her parents' fault for making her stay with them. She hadn't been able to say no.

Eventually, finally, she lifted herself off her bed and blinked repeatedly at the sun shining through her windows. Then, with mechanical movements, almost as though she had forgotten to act like a human, she made her way to the bathroom, turned on the shower, and let the hot water relax her tight body. She didn't know how long she was in there, but she ran out of hot water at some point, so she figured it was quite a while.

As Kate wrapped herself with a towel and found her way back to her bedroom, she realized she didn't even know what day it was. How long had she been in bed, wallowing listlessly in her state of depression? Suddenly, she realized she had been missing so much. She hadn't gone to school. She'd missed cheerleading practice and games. Her life had literally stopped. And now, she didn't even know if she could get back into her normal routine. Everything had changed.

Kate's mom had ironed her dress and had it hanging on the closet door by the time Kate got out of the shower. As Kate stood in front of the mirror, she realized how pale she was. It looked like she had lost ten pounds. Maybe she had. All of a sudden, she was famished. Her stomach began rumbling as she smelled the bacon cooking in the kitchen. Taking a deep, fortifying breath, Kate got dressed and stepped out of her bedroom for the first time in a week.

CHAPTER
4

Raelynn pulled to a stop after driving about a mile up the trail, which was not easily accessible from the main highway. The normal two-lane road slowly began to decline from gravel to more of a dirt path. Monte had taken crime scene tape and secured a large area that would be considered the crime scene. The yellow tape engulfed a large section of wooded area and a smaller clearing. This was out in the middle of nowhere, so crime scene tape may not have been strictly necessary, but procedures had to be followed.

Monte met Raelynn and Darla at the vehicle, ready with an update. "It's a white female, early twenties. She's been tied up. I would say that she hasn't been here long—maybe a few days, if that."

Well, there went the theory of a hunting accident. Speaking of which, the hunter who had found her was sitting on an overturned log just outside the tape boundary. From the look of it, the hunter hadn't seen too many dead bodies before. His face was ashen, and Raelynn guessed he may have vomited once or twice already.

Raelynn and Darla got out of the vehicle and started for the body. Darla had brought her coroner's bag and stopped just short of the yellow tape to pull on her white Tyvek suit to ensure no contamination of the evidence occurred during her preliminary examination. Then, she handed Raelynn a set of booties to pull over her shoes as well as a pair of rubber gloves.

Approaching the body, Raelynn could see that she was lying face up. Unable to repress her initial reaction, she gasped as the face of the victim came into view.

"Yeah, I know," Monte exclaimed sadly. "It's Katherine Williams. I definitely didn't want her name said over the radio."

Kate. That was what everyone knew her by. Raelynn's stomach churned, and she had to look away. She needed a moment to regain composure. Not just because she knew she was dealing with a homicide but because Kate worked at the local coffee shop, and she was a prominent figure in the community. Kate was the girl with the smile. She could befriend anyone. If someone was having a bad day, they could go get a cup of coffee from Kate and feel their whole day turn around. There was just something about her personality that made her feel like everyone's best friend. Customers always left the café in a better mood.

At first glance, Raelynn could just about confirm that this was the dumpsite. Kate lay there too neat and composed. It didn't appear any kind of struggle had occurred in the area. However, there were ligature marks around her ankles and wrists, making this an official homicide.

Upon initial observation, Raelynn couldn't identify a spot of blood, although there was a pretty grotesque bruise on the left side of Kate's face. The bottoms of her feet were almost black, probably from being barefoot for an extended period of time.

There were two aspects of this case that were quite profound right off the bat. First, Kate was clothed but barely—she was wearing a red lace nightie. Second, when Darla was in the middle of her examination, she located rose petals in the palm of her right hand.

Raelynn, her face somber and drawn, looked at Monte and Darla. "This isn't good," she muttered before taking a couple of steps back to allow Darla to proceed with her exam. Then, Raelynn turned to the officers. "Okay. Let's start a grid search and see what we can find. Mark anything—we don't know what's valuable and what isn't." After giving her orders, Raelynn made her way over to the distraught hunter, intent on finding some answers.

"Hi, I'm Detective Raelynn Bailey with the Seneca Rocks Police Department," she said in a polite but somewhat brisk tone. The man was pale as a ghost but shook Raelynn's outstretched hand. She took a seat beside him on the log to meet him on the same level. She never liked to approach an interview or interrogation presenting herself as having power over the individual. She instead learned early that if you create a rapport with the individual you are interviewing, they are more likely to open up and provide you with better intel. "So let's start with your basic information, shall we?" Raelynn continued, taking out a pad of paper to jot down notes.

The hunter nodded his head. "My name's Henry Cooper. I came up here to hunt."

"You related to the owner of Cooper's Store?" Raelynn asked.

"Yeah, Shawn's my cousin. He's who I stay with when I come into town to hunt. I live in New Jersey. There's nowhere to hunt there."

"So how long have you been coming here to hunt?" Raelynn assumed several years, as it takes an experienced hunter to navigate the Monongahela National Forest.

Henry smiled and said, "I've been hunting these woods since I was young. Usually grab me a big gobbler by now. Thought I was going to get lucky today. I'd been calling one, but it suddenly went quiet. I decided to move on up the trail a ways, and that's when I stumbled onto her."

Raelynn shook her head sadly. "Did you hear or see anyone else around?"

"No, I didn't see anyone, and I didn't hear anything either. That's the weird thing too. I mean, I didn't hear *anything*. Out here in the woods, you hear birds chirping and the smaller animals skittering about, but when I saw her, it was like the world paused. No sound at all." Henry shuddered and looked away, clearly spooked by the experience.

Raelynn knew exactly what he was talking about. It was like all the creatures could sense danger and went silent so they wouldn't be found. "We're gonna need you to come down to the station to fill out an official statement for us. I'll have one of the patrolmen take you back down. If you think of anything else, please give me a call."

Raelynn concluded the short interview by handing the hunter her business card. Then, she turned to Dane and asked him to take Mr. Cooper back to the station to give his official statement. Since Raelynn wanted to make sure that the chief had enough information to notify Kate's family, she further instructed Dane to comprehensively report what they had so far. "And please send up an ambulance so we can get the body to the morgue," she added.

With a deep sigh, Raelynn glanced over at the crime scene. Monte was busy taking photos, while Darla looked to be wrapping up her preliminary examination. The other officers were meticulously covering the crime scene on foot, following a grid pattern. One was walking east to west, while the others traveled north to south, trying to identify any potential clues.

In that brief moment of reprieve, Raelynn took a minute to step outside the yellow tape and get a good look at the scene. The fog had cleared away, and the sun was shining, trying to warm up the area. In a few hours, she would have to shed her jacket. She could hear the crunch of grass and twigs as the officers continued their search of the vicinity. It didn't look like the scene was disturbed. How might someone get a body up here? The trail would be the easiest way, but it didn't look like the trail had been marred by any tire tracks. Maybe there were houses or farms not too far from here they should check out. Raelynn made a mental note to ask Monte.

Darla was just getting a body bag out of the Explorer when Raelynn stepped up to take a closer look at the body. "I expect she's been here at least overnight," Darla stated. "Full rigor mortis has set in, and I'd guess she's been here at least twelve hours. I can't find any obvious cause of death, but I'll know more when I get her back to the morgue."

As Raelynn helped Darla transfer the body into the body bag, she found herself hoping the chief was delivering the bad news to Kate's family as gently as he could. Looking swiftly over the area, she noted that the other officers apparently hadn't found much. There were only a few evidence markers scattered around.

One in particular caught her attention. With a brisk sense of purpose, she walked over to the edge of the forest where a patrolman had marked a broken tree branch. It was a fresh break, twisting grotesquely toward the crime scene. *This could be a possible path the suspect took, or it may have nothing do with Kate's death and could just be a trail that deer navigate through*, Raelynn thought to herself. Either way, the break was recent, and she tucked this piece of information into her mind for future processing.

"Does anyone live around here?" Raelynn asked Monte.

"This far up the trail is pretty sparse, but I believe there's a vacant farm not too far from here. It's probably at least a quarter mile away. I doubt someone would have been able to carry a dead body the entire way from there. More than likely, they drove her up here and dumped her body."

Raelynn nodded vaguely but made yet another a mental note to follow up later. After checking that all the evidence had been tagged, photographed, and collected, everyone started to pack up and head back to the office. By this time, the chief had sent an ambulance up to retrieve the body. Darla decided to ride back with them and pick her car up at the station later.

On the way back to the station, Raelynn realized there was a road not too far from the trail. She took a detour down the road to see if she could get a grasp of where the vacant farm was located. The road was packed gravel, and she sent dust up as she traveled. After about a mile, she encountered a locked gate on her right. *Was this it?* Raelynn pulled up to gate and glanced around. No markings of any kind. She debated whether to take a chance and check it out or wait until she had evidence and a warrant.

"What the hell," Raelynn said to no one. Then, with a sense of reckless determination, she climbed out of the safety of the Explorer, shed her jacket, and shimmied up the gate.

Once safely on the other side, Raelynn started the hike up the dirt road. It looked like it hadn't been used in a while; there were deep divots in the dry mud, but they also hadn't experienced the typical amount of spring rainfall that year. Mindful of her footing, Raelynn kept walking, keeping a watchful eye around her, until she hit a clearing.

Glancing to her left and right, Raelynn noted several no trespassing signs stapled to various trees around the field. This was normal procedure. Owners around these parts were very protective over their farmland. They didn't want other hunters to grab "the big one" on private property.

Before she knew it, Raelynn found herself standing in a wide hayfield. In the distance stood an old barn, weathered and beaten from years of harsh winter weather. Wary as ever, Raelynn picked up the pace and headed straight to the woebegone structure. She was technically trespassing on this land, and although she had a badge, owners wouldn't hesitate to protect their property out here. She had to be extremely careful.

As she gazed at the barn, Raelynn experienced a strange sense of familiarity. She had lived here all her life but could not remember ever running across this property, yet it was like she sensed she had seen it before. How could she have never known it existed until now? Trying to focus on the task at hand, she shrugged off that tickle of recognition and trudged forward.

Raelynn's radio came to life just as she reached the barn. The unexpected interruption alarmed her, causing her to jump. Laughing a little at herself, she pulled the mic from her shoulder clasp and turned down the volume. Then, Raelynn turned away from the old barn and headed back down the dirt road. She'd make another trip back out here. She wanted to get a feel for how long it would take to walk from the barn to where Kate's body was found.

A theory was forming in her mind. If the trail hadn't looked like it had been used by motor vehicles, then Kate's body had to have gotten there some other way. Maybe this was the location where Kate's body had come from. Hopefully, Raelynn would be able to find the owner and make the next visit more official. She sure didn't want to give anyone a reason not to give her a search warrant, if needed.

Sure, right now, she just had a theory, but Raelynn put a lot of stock in her intuition, and her gut was telling her she was onto something. She just had to wait and see what else she could find out.

CHAPTER
5

Kate took her spot on the passenger side of his vehicle, then reached across the center console and placed a quick peck on his cheek. He was so handsome, and Kate felt lucky he had found her. Despite all that she'd gone through, she believed that her life was renewed. She lived every day consumed with the anticipation of seeing him. There was no doubt she hadn't felt like this for anyone since Adam. In fact, she'd pushed everyone away and struggled to meet the expectations that everyone placed on her.

Truth be told, people in the community hadn't helped her out in a good way. Of course, they didn't see it like that. Ever since Adam died, they'd treated her with pity. Suffocating in the depths of her sadness, Kate stopped caring about anything in her life, specifically school. She let her grades slide, but the teachers didn't seem to care. She still somehow graduated at the top of her class. Kate also started losing weight, but everyone claimed that was a normal thing to happen after experiencing a death. She heard the snickers behind her back. People would say one thing to her face—"oh, you're so pretty"—but as soon as she turned away, the truth about how they felt came out.

As a result, it was rather easy for Kate to keep her secret hidden. She wasn't open to starting a new relationship. Some of her friends would try to set her up on a date, but she wasn't interested. In fact, she wasn't interested in anything—except one thing.

She did, however, meet new acquaintances. That was all they were—people she needed to support her secret. It was pretty easy to score when and where she needed to. Luckily, Kate had gotten hired at the local coffee shop shortly before her secret habit emerged. Her easygoing personality put her at the top of the list to help manage. Often, she worked alone. No one suspected she arranged extra deliveries there.

Kate vividly remembered the first time she tried it. A guy had come into the café about an hour before it closed. He'd taken a seat at a back table and watched her work. At the same time, she'd watched him out of the corner of her eye. He had ordered a coffee, but based on her observations, he hadn't consumed a drop. As it got closer to the end of her shift, she approached the table and slid into the seat across from the guy.

"Hi, I'm Kate," she said with a shy smile.

"I know who you are. I hear you need some help," he replied.

"Need help? Who told you that?" she answered tightly.

He smirked at her. This was the typical response he got when he approached those in need. "It doesn't matter. I can tell by looking at you." The stranger slowly reached for her hand across the table. Still unsure but intrigued, she let him touch her—let him slide his fingers across her palm. "I can help you feel better. Help you with the pain and give you the strength to make it through the days."

Kate had to admit the offer sounded too good to be true. So without even giving it much thought, she nodded and stood up. Walking behind the bar, she grabbed her bag as he rose from the table, set aside his coffee cup, and walked out the door. Kate followed behind, shutting off the lights and locking up. When she turned back toward him, he was waiting by a black sedan, gallantly holding the passenger door open. She slid in. After getting behind the wheel, the stranger backed out of the lot and took her down by the river, where he parked the car.

At that point, Kate's anxiety began to kick in. Why was she in a car with a man she didn't know? She lunged for the door handle, but he grabbed her arm, preventing her from scampering away.

"Relax, I'm not going to hurt you," he said in a soothing tone. Before she could continue second-guessing the situation, the guy brought out a baggie half filled with a fine white powder. Catching her gaze, he licked his finger and stuck it in the bag. Kate watched as he lifted his finger to his nose and inhaled the substance. Then, he closed his eyes and tilted his head back, clearly in a state of utter relaxation.

After a moment, he rolled his head back toward her and smiled lazily. In a fluid motion, he dipped his finger back in the bag and offered it up to Kate. Without a moment's hesitation, she looked him in the eye and sniffed her new addiction from his finger.

The sudden surge of adrenaline shot through her body like a lightning bolt. Kate sat back and let the drug take effect. All her senses instantly went on edge, and she gripped the dash as the euphoria took over her body. She didn't know how long they sat in silence in the dark, but eventually, he started the car and drove back to the café.

"I'll be in touch," he stated as she opened the door to get out. Still in a state of deep relaxation, Kate watched him drive away as she stood in the parking lot. Tonight, her world had changed. It was too soon to tell the outcome, but she liked what she was feeling so far.

Kate didn't believe she had a problem. Sure, she seemed to frequently hear comments like, "Girl, you need to eat more" or "Why didn't you go on to the university?" But whenever anyone mentioned something like that to her, she played it off as still having issues with Adam's death. She used that excuse a lot.

And people didn't even know the true depth of what she was dealing with. Kate didn't want to admit she was hooked on heroin. She used it to numb the pain—the feeling of self-pity and regret. She found that it kept her alive or at least prevented her from falling into her deep sleeps. That's when Adam would visit her. In her dreams. They all ended the same—with him waving goodbye. She couldn't stand it, so she refused to go to sleep.

Despite her denial, the drug use was getting worse for Kate. She'd started by snorting it, but over time, it seemed that she'd become immune to it. That's when she began sneaking off to go down by the river. She wasn't proud of what she was doing, but there hadn't been other sources of help. Despite the fact that she lived in a community that was always in everyone's business, no one reached out a helping hand. This was the only way she could cope. Her drug use may not have been healthy, but at least it was getting her through, and that was more than she could say for anyone else in her life . . . at least before.

She felt different now that he'd found her and rescued her. The outcome could have been so different that day. He could have taken her to the police station. He could have found her dead. Instead, he'd wrapped his arms around her and rediscovered the old Kate. As she experienced for herself, it only took one person to make a difference in someone's life. He'd brought Kate into a whole new mindset.

At first, she wondered if he was just holding her secret over her head, sort of like blackmail to stay with him. However, she soon realized that he truly had feelings for her. Not long after he discovered her, little things started to happen in her life. Good things for a change. Flowers would arrive at the coffee shop. Each bouquet had red and pink flowers of some sort, usually either roses or tulips. He made sure no one knew who they were from. She displayed them on the bar and told everyone the place needed to have a bit of color. Every time she glanced at them, a smile would appear on her face.

As time went on, she found herself looking out the coffee shop's windows to see if he would drive by. She felt her heartbeat instantly increase when he came into the café to get his usual cup of coffee. She tried not to draw attention to her fascination with him, letting him socialize with the other customers like any other day, but she knew he was there because of her. As he left, he would always make sure he said goodbye and gave her a wink. There was no doubt his visits had become more frequent, so she sensed he couldn't get enough of her, just as she couldn't get enough of him. Then, he would pick her up after her shifts, and they would drive around the town, usually finding a spot to relax and make out.

Kate had been trying to quit the drugs since he'd found her. She wanted to be able to experience true feelings for him instead of the manufactured emotions the drugs made her feel, but she wasn't having much luck. She would tell him that her use had slowed down, but, in fact, it hadn't. She really did try to slack off, but each time she didn't keep her high, she would fall into her dreams. She couldn't deal with those yet. The drugs were the only way to forget about Adam and get on with her life.

She knew his routine, and the days he wasn't able to stop by allowed her to arrange special drop-offs. She would always find herself down by the river. She guessed it was a sentimental spot for her since it was the first place she had gotten high. Conscientious of her dependence, she was sure to acquire enough drugs to get her through this weekend without him knowing. She was very careful; no one even suspected she was using. Her parents assumed that since she worked the evening and night shifts at the café, that was why she was up the rest of the night. With her body screaming for sleep, Kate would nap on and off during the daytime hours to get by.

Feeling a rush of contentment, Kate snuggled back into her seat as he pulled the car out and started down the road. She was so excited. This was the first time they had been alone together for quite a while. She didn't know how he'd managed to pull it off, but he did.

"Lie back and relax," he said. "I know you have to be tired. I'll wake you when we get there." Kate smiled at him and took his advice.

Only moments later, or so it seemed, he gently touched her shoulder. Kate glanced around, but all was dark. "Where are we?" she asked, straining to make out anything in the pitch black.

He didn't respond.

Kate had expected that they would check into a hotel or bed and breakfast once they crossed the state line. "Are we lost?" She started to squirm in her seat, unsure of what was going on. She tried to look out the car windows, but all she saw was the dark sky. There didn't even seem to be one single star illuminating the way.

"We're here, but first, I have something for you," he stated as he reached into the back seat and handed her a bag. The bag itself was beautiful, tied up in all kinds of red ribbons and bows. He knew her favorite color was red.

Reassured, Kate began to relax again, letting the wariness subside. Sometimes, she just didn't know when to hold her tongue. Why should she be concerned? He wouldn't put her in harm's way. He was a natural protector. She trusted him.

Kate couldn't repress the big smile that crept across her face. She loved presents. Wanting to cherish this moment, she took her time unraveling the ribbons. Then, she carefully reached into the bag and felt a soft material. Tightening her hand around the fabric, she gently pulled it out of the bag.

"I want you to wear it for me. I know you will look beautiful in it," he explained as Kate held up a piece of crimson lingerie.

This was a first experience for her, and she felt herself blush. She'd never worn anything like this before. Up until this moment, the level of sexual interactions between them had maxed out at making out and some second base action. He was always a gentleman when they were together. Kate knew the desire was there for both of them, but he never pursued it. She wasn't naïve. She knew this weekend encounter would resolve many of their wants. But she was a bit taken aback by this blatant expression of his intentions for her.

Although she'd cast her eyes down in embarrassment, Kate felt his fingers trace down her cheek and gently comb through her hair. She would do anything to make him happy. As her embarrassment subsided in response to his intimate touch, Kate held up the nightie to get a better view of his gift. There wasn't much to it, which was typical, she supposed.

Kate leaned into his palm and gave him a shy smile. "I love it. Of course, I'll wear it for you."

"Wait here for a bit. I need to turn on some lights." With that, he left her alone in the car and started on his journey to their destination. Kate sat back and tried to focus on her surroundings. She still couldn't recognize anything. It looked like they were parked in a big field of some sort.

After a while, Kate's feeling of anticipation gave way to worry. She glanced at the clock in the dash. He had been gone for about fifteen minutes. Where could he have gone?

At this point, her eyes had had enough time to begin adjusting to the deep darkness. The sky was a bottomless blue, and stars were sparse, but she could now pick out a few across the vast expansion. Kate could also make out the faint outline of the moon hidden securely behind clouds. It was definitely not a full moon.

This week had been beautiful for early spring, with temperatures reaching sixty degrees during the day but dipping low enough at night for the ground to freeze. Tonight was one of those nights. Noticing the goosebumps raising the flesh on her arms, Kate wrapped her arms around her in a bear hug to protect herself from the chill. She wished she had brought a sweater or light jacket to overcome the chilliness.

Straining her eyes, she did her best to see into the darkness. Far away, she thought she saw a faint light. Was her mind just playing tricks on her? It seemed the light would flicker and go out, causing her to wonder if she was going crazy.

Kate's anxiety was truly setting in by this point. Where was he? She didn't have a clue where she was, and he had left her out there alone. Just as panic rose in her throat, her car door suddenly opened, causing her jump. Ignoring her startled reaction, he bent down and gave her a warm smile.

"Ready?" he asked, offering a hand. "It's just a little hike out through the field. Don't worry—I know the way and won't let you stumble."

Kate took the proffered hand and stepped out into the dark night, trying to release the concern that had been choking her moments before.

"What is this place?" she inquired as she fell into a slow pace beside him.

"It's been in the family for generations. A lot of people don't even know it's out here."

Kate noticed he was very cautious about sharing details. Didn't he trust her?

She knew a lot about him already—stuff that was known to everyone. It was no secret that he was married, but he'd assured Kate that his only love was her. He was just waiting until the right time to make it public. He didn't want to invoke people's disapproval—at least not without a plan for how to move forward. The community had placed high expectations on him, something Kate understood, as she had to contend with those expectations as well.

That's why she was content with meeting him in secret for the time being. It seemed fitting actually. One day, they would be together and would be able to tell everyone. She kept hoping it would be sooner than later though. Sometimes, she became pushy, especially if she hadn't been able to see him in a while. Of course, when she didn't see him, she substituted his absence with drugs. When she was high, she became paranoid about everything, but especially him. She always focused on the fact that he was with someone else when he wasn't with her. In turn, she'd confront him about how much she meant to him and urge him to be open with their relationship. But he was always so calm and eventually put her at ease every time.

Kate gripped his hand hard and slowly followed his lead. This was definitely a field. Kate could feel the wet grass grabbing at her pant legs. It felt as though she were walking through a graveyard and clammy hands were snatching at her, begging her to pull them from the ground. For some reason, she wanted to run, to swiftly move past this ominous setting, but he had a firm grasp on her hand. He was so strong—inescapable. Kate never feared anything while with him, but she also knew not to test his boundaries. Although he'd never laid a rough hand on her, she was sure he had the power to handily control others.

It didn't take long for the car to disappear from view. As they walked deeper into the darkness, Kate glimpsed the faint light up ahead. It definitely was light, not her eyes or imagination playing tricks on her. The longer she was in the dark, the more her eyes became accustomed to her surroundings. Although they were walking through a field, she could see the large pine trees lining the field. She had no idea how long she'd been traipsing by his side, one hand held firmly within his and the other gripping her present. She wasn't dressed for a hike through a field. Kate's lonely sweatshirt, worn and thin, let in the cold breeze, and she began to shiver. The hand on the present was starting to go numb, and she didn't know if it was from the cold or from the intense grip she had around the handles.

Gradually, the light grew. Again, Kate felt compelled to pick up the pace. At the same time, she felt herself yielding to tiredness. It was way past midnight, and she'd been awake for eighteen hours. All she wanted to do was go someplace warm and sleep.

As they drew closer to the light, Kate could barely see an outline of a large building. At first, she thought that he had rented a faraway cabin, but then, she remembered he'd said it was in the family. With nothing else to distract her, Kate focused her attention on deciphering their destination. It was a two-story structure with very few openings. It took her a few minutes, but then she realized that they had arrived at a barn. A barn? He'd promised her a romantic getaway, yet he'd brought her to a barn. Kate was not impressed.

He let go of her hand and grasped the door of the barn, which was standing ajar. Kate took a step back to let the door swing by, but he firmly grabbed her, almost as if she were trying to run away and he wanted to keep her in place.

"Ouch, you're hurting me!" Kate exclaimed as he pulled her toward the entrance.

"Sorry, I thought you were tumbling backward. I didn't want you to fall," he replied casually, but he didn't ease up on the pressure

around Kate's wrist. Instead, he pulled her through the door and into the openness of the desolate structure. A lone light was burning from a gas-fueled lantern beside a makeshift bed of hay. Strands of straw were trying to escape from underneath the blanket that had been draped on top. This was not a cabin in the woods as she had hoped from her first glimpse of the place. She had pictured them wrapped in each other's arms, maybe even lounging in a hot tub. But there was certainly no hot tub here.

Kate took a moment to let her eyes adjust to her surroundings. This had to be a joke. There was no way that this was what he had planned for them. This was not romantic at all—it was horrendous! Even the random flings that Kate had had in high school had been more considerate than this, and those had been hormone-induced quickies from teenage boys.

Struck anew with a feeling of unease, Kate took a measured step away from him. This time, he let go of her wrist and allowed her to walk around freely. There wasn't much else in the barn. It seemed to be partitioned off into sections. Maybe it had been used as horse stalls or to separate yearlings from the mothers. The barn wood was weathered grey. The ceiling was low. She felt she could reach out and touch it. It smelled of damp hay, and Kate realized it wasn't much warmer compared to the outside. After strolling around the lone room, she cautiously wrapped her arms around her still chilly body.

"Why are we here?" Kate turned back to him, a wave of worry starting to build up in her stomach. She wanted to take a hit. She couldn't believe this was happening. Her anxiety was at an all-time high.

"I wanted to bring you someplace quiet so we could spend time together," he stated simply.

"I really didn't have this in mind. I was thinking more of a cabin, but a barn never crossed my mind."

"I knew this was one place no one would ever suspect. We are entirely alone. Isn't that what you wanted?" he asked Kate, leaning up against the closed barn door. He was very broad shouldered and took up much of the door frame. Something about the way he was leaning against the door definitely made her think he wanted to be in control.

She got the impression that he didn't want her to leave. After glancing around once more, she realized there were no other doors in this room. She was trapped. But she didn't know why she felt like this. She loved this man. He wouldn't hurt her. Right?

Overcome by the cold, or perhaps coming off her last hit, Kate started to shiver harder. She hadn't been prepared to spend the night in a barn without heat. Apparently recognizing her discomfort, he reached out and took her in his arms, leading her over to the makeshift bed.

"Here, you lay down and cover up for a bit," he advised. Needing no further encouragement, Kate sat down on the bed and placed her present on the floor. He flopped down beside her and retrieved a hidden thermos from the other side of the bed. After smoothly opening the container, releasing a welcome aroma, he let her sip on the warm coffee with his arms tight around her. Finally thawing out a little bit, Kate nuzzled her head under his chin. Despite the less-than-romantic surroundings, she felt so safe in his arms. She always felt safe with him.

As the cozy pair chitchatted about their day, Kate could feel the coffee begin to warm her up. Finally, warm and content, Kate nodded off.

When she awoke, she noticed he was not on the bed with her anymore. Slightly disoriented as the fog of sleep lifted, she tried to sit up but promptly realized she couldn't move her arms. Bewildered, Kate lifted her head as much as possible to try to see what was going on, glancing frantically to her left and right. To her surprise, both of her arms were held down to the floorboards with zip ties secured around her wrists.

What is happening? *She had to be dreaming. This couldn't be real.*

Trying not to panic, Kate attempted to lift her legs. They were bent at the knees, but she still couldn't move them very much. She realized that her shoes had been removed—she was barefoot. The longer she lay there, disoriented and confused, the more it dawned on her what was happening. Suddenly desperate, Kate tried to move any way she could. She arched her back, but her feet kept sliding out from under her on the cold, dirty floor. Rather than loosening her binds, her frantic movements seemed to be causing the zip ties around her wrists to get tighter, cutting painfully into her flesh.

As she lay there, panting and weeping, Kate's anxiety started to kick into high gear. Her heart beat faster and faster as any hope that this was a terrible nightmare faded. What is happening? Where did he go? Who's done this to me? *So many unanswered questions galloped through her mind, triggering a sense of deep dread. She'd known something didn't feel right about this place.*

As Kate continued squirming, fruitlessly trying to release herself from the grasp of the zip ties, the blanket slipped away from her body. She instantly halted her movements, horrified by the realization that something had changed. The last thing she remembered was falling asleep in his arms, the present presumably forgotten beside the bed. Now, Kate was no longer wearing her sweatshirt and jeans. Instead, she had the red lingerie on.

How did this happen?

Kate's mind grappled with the severity of her circumstances. All she'd wanted was some alone time with the man she loved. She just wanted to have him all to herself. How had she let things spiral so far out of control? What was going to happen next? She didn't like kinky sex, and she certainly hadn't been aware that he was into this type of stuff.

Overwhelmed with emotion and exhausted from her efforts to free herself, Kate stopped struggling. Almost as soon as she resigned herself to her position, she heard someone outside the barn. Should she yell for help? What were the chances that was actually someone coming to rescue her? She didn't even know where she was. As fear began to overcome Kate, tears rapidly welled up in her eyes.

Before she could compose herself, the door began to rattle and slowly swung open. He walked in and methodically approached her as if she were a timid animal. Kate looked at her captor, hurt and betrayal in her eyes. She would never have guessed he would put her through something like this. Still barely able to move, she followed his movements around the perimeter of the room, noting the light from the lantern flashing shadows across his face. With unsettling swiftness, he abruptly approached and knelt down beside her. She could smell him; his cologne was suddenly overpowering.

"I told you that you would look beautiful in that lingerie," he remarked casually as his eyes roamed over her body. Kate's breathing increased, and she began to feel a crushing sense of hopelessness. When he sat down beside her, she actually tried to get away from him, but it was no use. As she struggled, her feet continued slipping out from under her. The barn wood sent tiny needles of wood through her bare feet, which were already streaked with dirt. She couldn't escape. He gave a slight chuckle as he watched her wrestle with the bindings.

He stroked her face with his hand and continued down her body, touching every part of her. It was like he was making an image using his hands—as if he wanted to remember every part of her by using the sense of touch. Kate closed her eyes as he leisurely traced her form, starting with her eyes. He was meticulous as his hands roamed across her, gradually making their way down to her stomach and eventually stopping as he stroked each toe.

As the magnitude of the circumstances fully impressed upon Kate, she began to cry uncontrollably, her guttural sobs growing louder and louder. Suddenly, he sat up straighter and, using the back side of his hand, struck her across the cheek. This sudden change in him startled Kate into silence, her sobs dying with a faint hiccup. He had never hit her before. He had always been so gentle. Of course, she'd never been in this predicament before either. He still hadn't shouted at her. All it took was him hitting Kate across the face to regain control.

"You know, we had a good thing," he murmured. Kate remained silent, afraid that he would hit her again. "You just had to go and fall in love with me," he sighed, not directly looking at her face.

Kate tried to regain composure. She couldn't let the tears and fear overwhelm her, but she couldn't find the words to respond.

"You see, we could never be together," he continued casually. "You were someone who needed help. That's what I do—I help people. And I liked the attention. I don't get much of that at home. You were just meant to occupy my time. I also liked being with you. It makes me hard just thinking about getting some from such a young girl."

Kate made no response, letting him talk. As he continued with his monologue, a seed of outrage bloomed in her mind, but she was too frightened to examine it too closely. She couldn't believe what she was hearing.

"And I'm finally going to get it this time. Don't worry—you won't feel a thing. I just wanted to see you in your new present. You like it, don't you?"

It was a question, but Kate knew she didn't have to answer. At this point, he was just talking out loud, not really to her directly. She kept watching him as his gaze lingered on her body. To her horror, he reached behind him and retrieved a syringe. Kate's eyes were wide open now. She hadn't said anything for several long moments, but fear instantly overcame her at this point, and the questions started to flow.

"Why are you doing this? Can't we just forget about all this, and you let me go?" Kate whispered, keeping an eye on the syringe. Still, she tried to get away, but her bound arms wouldn't allow her to move.

"Oh, beautiful Kate," he began. "You are so naive. You know we can't continue this relationship. I won't let you destroy what I have accomplished."

Kate started to whimper, the harsh reality of her situation sinking in even deeper. "How about just letting me go?" she pled again in a broken voice. "I promise not to tell anyone. We can both go on with our lives."

This made him laugh out loud. "You're so sure that no one will find out, huh? We live in too small a community. Someone will find out eventually. I can't let that happen." He grabbed her arm suddenly. "It's so easy to give a lethal dose of a drug to an IV drug user. No one will expect anything else once they see all the track marks on your skin."

With no mercy, he pinned down her arm on the barn floor. He was so strong that it was useless for Kate to try to struggle against his control. Before she could make any move to stop him, he injected the clear liquid into her body. Kate gasped as she felt the drug race through her veins. It went straight through to her heart. Within seconds, her body became sluggish and heavy. She tried to move but realized she was pervasively numb. The drug was paralyzing her, yet she was completely aware of her surroundings—she could see, hear, and smell everything around her. The urge to scream was overwhelming, but she couldn't open her mouth. There was no better definition of torture.

Her body continued to spiral out of her control, but Kate could still see him sitting beside her, a slight grin crossing his face. She watched as he moved lower down her body—first his eyes, then his hands. Betraying no trace of hesitation or regret, he gripped her legs and spread them as far apart at the tiedowns allowed.

She couldn't move. She knew what was going to happen, but she couldn't stop it. With tears slowly crowding her eyes, she watched as he unbuckled his pants and pulled them down below his knees. Then, he knelt before her, lifting her slightly off the ground.

She closed her eyes against the horrific sight in front of her as a single tear escaped and slid down her face. The man she loved was now raping her. She didn't know how long it lasted. Time stood still at this point. But at least she was numb and couldn't fully feel what she was going through. Through the haze of drugs and denial, Kate could hear his low moans of pleasure and knew when he had finished.

After a while, Kate opened her eyes. He had removed the zip ties from her legs and arms, yet she was still unable to move. All she could do was watch as he picked her up and carried her out of the barn.

It was early morning, with the sun barely above the horizon. The sky was still a deep gray. Kate could no longer see the stars or the moon. All she saw was sky. He walked with her body lying loose as a rag draped over him, but she seemed heavy as dead weight. Listless and dull, she watched as they passed the pine trees that she had spotted the night before on their way to the barn. She could hear his breath become labored as he climbed through the dense vegetation. In fact, he stopped a few times on the trek to catch his breath. Finally, after what felt like an eternity, he placed Kate on the ground. She was only aware of the change when the sky stopped moving, but she was still staring at the endless gray.

Almost in a ritualistic manner, he placed her hands palms together over her stomach. Kate watched helplessly as he reached into his back pocket and pulled out a single rose. Red. Again, her favorite. Then, he plucked several petals from it and placed them inside her palms.

Clearly unburdened by any manner of sadness, he remained with her only a few minutes more. She knew that being with him had been entirely an illusion on her part. It had been nothing but a big—deadly—game for him. He didn't love her.

Kate was left alone. Far from friends, far from family, far from anyone. Finally, finally, *she closed her eyes and prayed to go see Adam.*

CHAPTER 6

Raelynn decided to grab a quick lunch of her normal cheeseburger and fries at the local diner. Fortunately, word hadn't gotten out yet about Kate, so her meal went pretty smoothly. She wasn't ready to field questions yet—she simply didn't know enough. Plus, she was still processing the whole situation. Anyway, now was the time to listen to people. She'd learned from experience that she could find out so much more information by just sitting and listening.

The diner was one of those traditional mom-and-pop joints. Large windows overlooked a parking lot. The outside of the building showed nothing remarkable. Other than the sign outside directing visitors to the right location, nothing stood out to identify it as a restaurant. The diner had been around for as long as Raelynn could remember. Now in the second generation of ownership, it remained essentially the same as the opening day. Not much had changed except for the installment of some newer booths—the same color as the originals—inside.

As a teenager and through college, Raelynn had actually worked there as a weekend waitress, so she was intimately familiar with the establishment. The diner offered daily specials, but everything was homemade, right down to the desserts. One of her favorites was the butterscotch pie with meringue piled a mile high. Of course, she had to control herself or she would gain fifty pounds.

The owners knew she worked on a tight schedule, so her meal was delivered in a timely fashion. As she was eating, Raelynn replayed the day's events in her mind. Only a few hours into one of the town's largest crimes, and she was stumped. *Why was the dumpsite in such a remote area? How did Kate get there?*

Raelynn paid her tab and hopped back into the Explorer. It had been a few hours since they had left the crime scene. She knew Darla would have started on her initial investigation of the body right away, and Raelynn was chomping at the bit to see what she'd uncovered.

Darla was relatively new at being the town's coroner, but she had been pursuing a career as a nurse ever since they'd graduated high school. Darla had known what she wanted to do with her life since she was a little girl. It was something Raelynn had always admired about Darla as they'd grown up together.

Darla was more than just a coworker—she was a true friend and confidante. She had been with Raelynn the entire time Raelynn's mother was battling cancer, demonstrating her natural talent as a nurse and nurturer. Often, Raelynn would find herself watching Darla take care of her mom, urging her to eat or helping her to the bathroom. It inspired a strange sense of gratitude and respect mixed with self-flagellation. Raelynn didn't have those skill sets in her.

It was hard for Raelynn to watch her mother suffer for so long. The cancer diagnosis had come when Raelynn was in high school. Sure, she had noticed that her mother spent a lot of time sleeping, but as a teenager, it wasn't at the top of Raelynn's priority list. The summer of her junior year, the doctors said that a tumor had taken over a large part of her mother's brain. Distraught beyond belief, Raelynn thought her world would shatter. That entire summer, Raelynn camped out by her mother's bedside, often with Darla. She watched as her mother lost more and more of her life every day. By the end of September, her mother's only response was her shallow breathing. She hadn't been awake for days. Raelynn was holding her hand as she slipped away.

Raelynn stepped through the sliding glass doors of Seneca Rocks Hospital. Perhaps it was surprising because of her job title, but she disliked hospitals. It was the smell that got her. That aroma of disinfectants brought back bad memories. Memories she didn't want to relive.

Repressing a shudder, Raelynn walked by the receptionist, pushed the down button on the elevator, and waited impatiently for the doors to open. Once inside, she pressed the button for the morgue. The ride was short, and the elevator doors opened to reveal a long hallway. Although the walk to the exam room where Darla performed her autopsies wasn't far, the further she went, the more she smelled sanitizers mixed with the undeniable scent of death. It was a smell that one couldn't mistake.

Scrunching her nose in distaste, Raelynn pushed open the exam room door and grabbed a mask and gloves from the side table. Darla was talking into a small tape recorder and held up a finger to indicate she would be done in a moment. Once finished, Darla tucked the recorder into the pocket of her lab coat and turned to Raelynn.

"Well, let's get started, shall we?"

Raelynn nodded her head and placed a dab of Vicks vapor rub under her nose. Whatever she could do to hide the smell.

Darla chuckled and commented, "You know that just opens your senses more, right?"

Shrugging, Raelynn replied, "It makes my mind calmer during this." With a quirk of her eyebrows, she motioned to Darla to proceed.

Raelynn looked down at Kate. Even in death, she was a beauty. She lay on the stainless-steel examination table with her eyes closed and the common v-cut across her chest, as Darla had already performed her autopsy. A white sheet was pulled up to her waist. She looked like she was sleeping. Who could have done this? Everyone knew Kate had her issues, and some had even suggested she had a drug problem. She had gone through a very difficult time when her high school boyfriend, Adam, had passed away, but it seemed that over the last six months she had begun pulling herself out of the slump.

"First, I examined the outside of the body, and I didn't find much more than what I already knew from when she was at the crime scene. There are ligature marks around both her ankles and wrists. From the indentation, it looks like she was tied up with either cables or possibly even zip ties. Definitely not rope—she didn't have any rope burns. It doesn't look like she was tied up for long though because the marks aren't deep. The skin isn't broken—just bruised."

Raelynn pondered for a moment. "Does she have any defensive wounds on her?"

"That's the funny thing," Darla responded. "I didn't find any. I took scrapings from under her fingernails, but her knuckles don't have any abrasions on them. So it looks like she didn't try to fight her attacker. The only bruise I could find was the one on her face. It looks like it was from a fall or maybe being held down. Also, she had no broken bones."

The savvy coroner explained the expansive purple bruising on her back was actually livor mortis, which occurred when the blood settled to the lowest part of her body. With no other bruising or broken skin on the outside of the body, Darla ruled out the possibility that a beating had taken place. From her thorough observations, it looked like Kate hadn't struggled with her assailant. This made her death even more strange. Why wouldn't she have fought back? Could she have known her killer?

"I drew blood and sent it off to toxicology. My initial guess is that she died from hypothermia, but I won't know until I get the results back." This was a reasonable assumption, as the temperature at night could get down to freezing. Given what Kate had been found in—the red lingerie—her body temperature could have easily dropped quickly. But this just opened up more questions for Raelynn. *Was she unconscious outside? She had to have been drugged or unconscious in order to lay there long enough to die.*

Darla walked around the examination table so she could look her friend in the face. "You're not going to like what else I found out."

Raelynn's stomach sank. That was never a good sign.

"Did you know Kate used drugs?" Darla asked.

"I heard the rumors. It sounded like it started after Adam died," Raelynn responded.

"Based on my observations, she wasn't what we would consider a recreational user. You know, using to fit in or while at a party. Raelynn, she has visible track marks."

Darla reached out and rotated Kate's arms. Raelynn could feel her mouth drop open. It was apparent Kate was a perpetual IV user. Her arms clearly showed the path of use. Darla grabbed the white sheet covering the lower portion of Kate's body and pulled it up to cover the evidence of the autopsy. Raelynn wondered how many people actually knew about her drug use.

"I also identified signs that she had sex recently."

"So she was sexually assaulted?" Raelynn asked.

"Not necessarily. That's why I said she had sex recently. There are no signs of trauma to her genital area. It looks like any sexual activity could have been consensual," Darla explained.

Raelynn took a step back and found a stool to sit on. "So let me recap for a moment. Kate has no signs of trauma on her body other than the ligature marks, and you're saying she had sex recently. Allegedly consensual."

Darla nodded in affirmation.

With a sigh, Raelynn continued. "First instinct is that Kate knew her killer, unless she really wasn't killed. Maybe she just died, and this person got scared and had to get rid of her body?

Or maybe Kate was in a consensual relationship at first, and it turned more aggressive? This would explain the bondage and the lingerie that she was wearing." She had numerous theories running through her head.

Raelynn was asking a lot of questions aloud, but Darla didn't respond to any—just listened. She knew Raelynn wasn't actually directing any of these questions at her but just throwing them out in general. Darla waited patiently, allowing her friend to verbally think through scenarios.

"What about her feet? Why are they so dark?" wondered Raelynn.

Darla half-heartedly shrugged her shoulders. "They're just covered in dirt. Maybe she walked somewhere without her shoes. But I did notice she had some splinters in her feet. They may have been there from some other time, but I wouldn't think so. Splinters hurt, especially if they're in your feet."

Raelynn barely bothered to respond, lost in thought over the facts they'd gathered so far. She really needed those toxicology results back. That could shed a lot of light on the unknowns that remained shrouded in darkness.

"I'll email you the full report in a day or two," Darla stated. She was antsy to examine the toxicology results as well.

With a deep sigh, Raelynn stripped off her gloves and mask as she left the cold examination room and tossed them in the trash. The chief wasn't going to like this.

Raelynn stepped out into the fresh air outside the hospital. After wiping the Vicks out of her nostrils, she took several deep gulps of fresh, cleansing air. The sun was shining full force. No one would suspect that such a tragic event could happen on such a beautiful day.

Her lips forming a grim line, Raelynn glanced around the hospital parking lot before heading back to the station. She knew the chief would be expecting an update and that he would have notified Kate's family by now. Surely the horrific news would start spreading around town like wildfire soon enough. She owed it to Kate and her family to get some answers.

CHAPTER 7

Upon arriving at the station, Raelynn walked through the squad room doors and went straight to the chief's office. His disposition didn't seem to have improved over the course of the day; he looked like someone had just run over his dog. In fact, he was visibly upset, which was very unnatural for him.

"You okay, Chief?" Raelynn knew it was a stupid question, but it flew out of her mouth before she could contain it.

Chief Austin just looked at her and, instead of acknowledging her inane question, said, "Fill me in on what you have."

Without preamble, Raelynn told the chief everything she knew up to that point, specifically what Darla had discovered during her examination. The one detail she left out was her hike out to the barn. She thought that should remain undisclosed until she could get more proof. Besides, that was only a hunch.

Chief Austin had been in this business too long and wasn't a dumb man. The frown on his face just confirmed that he was thinking the same as Raelynn: Kate new her assailant. This was definitely something they had to explore.

"What are you planning next, Detective?" This was the first big investigation for Raelynn in this responsible role. She knew a lot was riding on this.

"Well, I want to retrace Kate's last whereabouts and see if there was anything out of the ordinary. Plus, talk to her coworkers and family, of course." Raelynn figured someone would know something, but that meant making her death known to the public.

Chief Austin sighed. "I told her parents a couple of hours ago. Give them some time before you go questioning them. Let the shock wear off."

Raelynn agreed and left to go to her office. Before she started any line of questioning, she wanted to get more familiar with the victim, and in today's society, the best way to do that was social media. So she sat hunched at her computer and loaded the internet.

It didn't take long to find Kate's Facebook page. It was only semi-private, and it provided some pictures and a few public comments. However, there wasn't much to see on her Facebook profile, so Raelynn promptly switched over to Instagram, where Kate had apparently been much more active.

Kate had been such a pretty girl. It was easy to see that she was usually the center of attention in a crowd. Raelynn cruised through Kate's posts but couldn't find a single picture of her with any particular guy, not even Adam. Maybe after Adam's death, she'd deleted all the memories. The rest of Kate's profile didn't provide anything of value either. The typical stuff was on there, such as the high school she'd attended, her birthdate, and the fact that she was "interested in men."

Recognizing she would have to get more information to make any breakthroughs in the case, she called for one of the officers in the squad room. When he poked his head into her office, she tasked him with getting a search warrant for Kate's social media accounts and messages.

For the next phase, Raelynn pulled up Google Maps and searched for the Seneca Creek Trail. She needed to find that farm and see how close it was to the crime scene. It took Raelynn a good half hour to locate what she thought was the property. It was further away than Monte had thought—more like a half mile.

Tapping her finger thoughtfully against her bottom lip, Raelynn reflected that she needed to know who that farm belonged to. Monte might know who owned the property, but he was out getting the pictures developed from the crime scene. So she'd just have to be patient and wait for the right time to ask him more questions about the farm. In the meantime, Raelynn would do the next best thing and head over to the courthouse to visit the county clerk in the record room.

This adventure didn't take long, as the courthouse was across the street from the police station. The county courthouse was a three-story building encased in old rock that had withstood the changes of time. Gradually over the years, the courthouse had been updated with the latest security systems, meaning a metal detector was installed at the main entrance. Although the security devices were in place, they were rarely used in a town of this size. The only time staff plugged in the metal detector was for grand juries or elections. Raelynn breezed right through without the faintest sound announcing her appearance.

She wasn't overly enthused with the response she received from the county clerk. Unfortunately, there was only one, and the process to get requested information would take some time. The clerk assured Raelynn that he would look into her request within the next week! This was not the most ideal scenario, but there wasn't anything Raelynn could do but wait for the pieces to fall into place. She wasn't even sure whether the farm was part of the puzzle; she just figured it didn't hurt to cover her bases.

Shaking her head in aggravation, Raelynn left the courthouse empty-handed but was determined to find some relevant piece of information before the day was through. So far, she was zero for two with her investigative skills.

The sun was starting to set over the mountaintops by the time Raelynn pulled into The Roast, the local coffee shop. She was lucky—she still had about an hour before they closed. During the week, their business hours were shorter. Raelynn hoped the owner, Mickey Marks, was working. He'd opened his coffee shop about ten years previously at a time when coffee shops were a new concept. For being located in such a small town, his coffee shop had really taken off. Townspeople preferred to buy local, whether it was fresh farm eggs from a neighboring farm or coffee.

Interestingly, Mickey was not someone one would necessarily expect to be running a coffee shop. Some people described him as flamboyant; others said he was just strange. Put simply, Mickey could be considered a pretty man. He took his appearance very seriously, from his wardrobe to his haircut. Each day, Mickey made sure his attire consisted of a brightly colored shirt and pressed khakis. He wore his hair short in the back and spiky on the top—certainly a unique style. The tips of his hair were always color coordinated with his shirt of the day.

Although Mickey did seem a bit odd, he ran a tight ship when it came to his coffee shop. He'd gotten the idea to open the joint when he'd traveled to Colombia, South America, during a missionary trip. He'd become intrigued with the process of roasting coffee beans and decided to make it his dream adventure when he returned to Seneca Rocks. With strong entrepreneurial sensibilities and a true passion for his work, Mickey only hired individuals that he felt confident would share his enthusiasm for coffee. His entire operation was run by six people, including baristas and coffee grinders. Kate had been an employee with the coffee shop since she had graduated high school.

Raelynn pushed open the coffee shop's door, drawing in a deep breath of roasted coffee, and quickly noted that she was the only one in the place. As she approached the counter, Mickey came from the back.

"Detective Bailey, it's awful late for you to get your usual," Mickey quipped.

"I'm not here for coffee, Mickey. I need to discuss something with you." Raelynn motioned to a nearby table, and Mickey pulled out a seat and joined her.

"I don't know how to tell you this, but we found a body up the Seneca Creek Trail."

Mickey simply stared at her, his face not registering anything.

"Mickey, it was Kate. We're investigating it as a homicide."

At the mention of Kate's name, Mickey's face became distorted. Raelynn was pretty good at reading people, but even she couldn't tell whether Mickey's reaction was shock, anger, or grief. It could have been a combination.

"I came here not only to tell you but to also ask you some questions."

Quite abruptly, Mickey pushed his chair back and stood up. Raelynn let him, recognizing he needed some time to comprehend the situation. Apparently needing the comfort of routine, Mickey walked behind the counter and made himself a cup of coffee. Then, he reached under the counter, retrieved a bottle of Irish whiskey, and added a good helping to his drink. With a brief gesture, he offered to make her a cup too, but she shook her head. Keeping his eyes cast down, Mickey took his time returning to the table, and when he finally sat, Raelynn could see that he was starting to tear up. "What can I help you with?"

Raelynn pulled out a notebook and pen to make some notes; however, she doubted she would actually jot anything down. Sometimes, taking notes was a distraction that prevented a meaningful conversation from taking place. "When was the last time you saw Katherine Williams?"

"Kate," Mickey corrected. "Everyone called her Kate. She went on vacation a couple of days ago. She was supposed to return tomorrow."

"Was it normal for her to take a vacation?" Raelynn asked.

"Actually, now that you mention it, this was the first official vacation that she asked for since starting here." Mickey scratched absently at the side of his head. "I always gave her the holidays off and if she seemed like she needed a break."

"Did she mention what she was going to do while on vacation? Maybe visit someone or travel some place?"

"Not really." He shrugged, looking almost guilty. "I asked her once if she had anything fun planned, and she said nothing extraordinary, but she had this smile on her face as she said it. I figured it wasn't something she wanted to share with her boss. She did seem more active on her phone lately. That's typically not like her. It was like she was afraid to put it down because she might miss something."

Raelynn's eyebrows knit together. "Do you know if Kate had a boyfriend or was interested in someone?"

Mickey laughed at that one. "You're not serious, right? It was more the other way around. Every man that walked through that door had a crush on Kate. And she flirted with everyone. That's how she got all her tips. Who would have thought a coffee shop could attract so much attention?"

"Was there anyone in particular you can remember who had an interest in Kate?"

Mickey shook his head regretfully. "Honestly, no one stands out. I mean, even Monte flirted with her. She really got to him actually. He would tip big time and come in a couple of times a day."

Raelynn laughed. No wonder Monte was so high strung. Drinking more than one cup of Mickey's coffee would definitely keep someone up at night.

"You said you would give Kate a day off if you could tell she needed a break," said Raelynn. "What do you mean by that?"

"Oh, well, sometimes Kate just seemed disconnected at work. I took it that I was working her too much, you know? So I would tell her to leave early and go home. I noticed sometimes that she would just say that she needed some fresh air and go for a walk. Eventually, when I looked outside, her car would be gone. Then, she'd show up the next day all refreshed. I didn't think much about it." Mickey shrugged again, that slightly guilty look casting a shadow on his face once more.

Raelynn just shook her head in reply. She understood Mickey not paying too much attention, and she understood Kate needing to take off sometimes. Even helping run a coffee shop could get stressful. Raelynn was much too familiar with taking a mental day to judge.

"Well, if you can think of anything that may be helpful, give me a call, will ya, Mickey?" Raelynn knew she wouldn't get any more information from him right now. The shock of the news would wear off soon, and she didn't want to be around for the tears.

With a sympathetic smile, Raelynn stood and made her way to the door. As she left, Mickey turned the closed sign on the door. Then, she saw him sit back down at the table with his coffee.

I feel ya, she thought to herself as empathy gripped her. Shitty ending to a day for sure.

CHAPTER 8

Detective Bailey felt her jaw unclench as she pulled gratefully into the driveway of her ranch-style house. She was exhausted. All she wanted to do was grab a beer and take a long bubble bath.

Raelynn lived in her parents' house. She had inherited it after their passing. Raelynn was an only child, and she couldn't bear to part with the house. Actually, she really hadn't changed much since she'd moved back in. Other than some new curtains and bedding, the house remained largely untainted by time or progress.

Moving her head from side to side to work out the kinks in her neck, Raelynn opened the refrigerator and looked inside. Besides the alcohol, her fridge was mostly empty. She really needed to fix more meals at home instead of eating at the diner all the time. *Oh well.* She grabbed a bottle of beer, twisted off the cap, and took a long, satisfying drink. *Man, that was good.*

Tossing the cap in the trash, she made her way down the hallway toward the bathroom. Intent upon pursuing her moment of self-care, Raelynn started the hot water and began to undress.

Then, she slipped into the warm bath water, her cold beer still secure in her hand. She hadn't had a day like this before, and, fingers crossed, she wouldn't have a day like this again. As Raelynn melted into the layer of bubbles, she closed her eyes.

She was walking down the hallway. She couldn't make out where she was, but she definitely smelled something familiar. The scent of cleanliness. Why do they have to make it smell like that? *Then, the scene changed, and Raelynn saw herself at the bottom of a bed. There were tubes going everywhere, and that smell became even more pungent. She stood watching as people came in and out of the room. It looked like they were busy, but she couldn't figure out what they were doing. She kept gazing at the bed, willing the image to get clearer, but it never did.*

Suddenly, Raelynn jerked awake and sat up. Her pulse was going a hundred miles per hour. She hated having that dream. Dang it—she needed to stop bringing her beer to the tub. Glancing over, she noted the bottle laying on the floor, liquid gold forming a pool that slowly inched closer and closer to the bathmat. What a waste of a good beer. One of these days, she was gonna drown by falling asleep in the tub.

Pursing her lips, she quickly rinsed off and grabbed a towel. Then, she put on shorts and a T-shirt and climbed into bed. Tomorrow would be a better day. Raelynn closed her eyes and willed herself to sleep soundly without the specter of the dreadful dreams.

Raelynn found herself walking down the hall again, except this time, she opened a different door. The sign on it said exam room three. Where had she seen that lately? *A hand reached out and touched the stainless-steel door. It was cold—extremely cold. The hand pushed on the frigid door slowly. As it nudged open, Raelynn took a step into the room, and the image came flooding back to her. She was in the morgue. There was that smell again—disinfectant. Raelynn felt as if she were floating. This time, she saw an exam table, not the usual hospital bed. As she drew closer, she felt certain that Kate would be lying on the table. Sweet, young Kate. Instead, Raelynn looked down and realized it was herself occupying the slab. She raised her hand to her mouth to stifle a scream . . .*

Raelynn bolted upright in her bed, glancing frantically around to make sure it had just been a dream. She was really in her bed in her home—safe. But she was soaked in sweat from head to toe. Raelynn had never had that dream before. Since the accident, she'd repeatedly endured the same nightmare. Always standing at the foot of the hospital bed and not clearly seeing who was occupying it. Tonight, her dream had obviously gone further.

Raelynn pulled back the covers and looked at the alarm clock. It was five thirty in the morning. Close enough to her wake-up time to get up and get ready for the day. She knew there was no way she would get back to sleep anyway. She might as well hit the street running this morning.

With a groan, Raelynn swung her legs over the side of the bed and stood up. She was already a sweaty mess from the dream, so she figured she may as well go for a run. She needed a way to shake the cobwebs from her head. Without changing out of her T-shirt and shorts, she slid her feet into her tennis shoes.

Moments later, as she stepped out onto her porch, she noted the sun was fighting to rise. Pinks and oranges stained the clouds, steadily lightening the deep blue of the sky above. Eager to escape her demons, she took a deep breath and took the first step of her run.

CHAPTER
9

How much shittier could Abby's day—or last few days—get? First, Abby's husband, Nate, had discovered the clandestine online relationship that she was conducting. Abby planned on leaving Nate eventually, but the huge fight had caused her to leave early and abruptly without a firm strategy in place.

Naturally, Nate had been infuriated. He had every right to be upset. Abby could understand that. However, Nate refused to open his eyes to the reasons why Abby had gotten involved with someone else. Nate worked every day. If he wasn't working as the foreman in the mines, he was working as a handyman for everyone else's needs—except hers.

Nate and Abby had met in high school and had been together ever since. That's what happens in small towns in Kentucky. People don't leave. They stay and get sucked into their new life of despair. Abby could readily admit that Nate provided financially for them. No question about that. However, Nate wasn't affectionate, and that was what Abby craved. She just needed someone to appreciate her. To say thank you after preparing all the meals, doing the laundry, and keeping the house. Since Abby didn't work, she made sure that all of Nate's needs were met.

Nate had no qualms about telling her that he wasn't going to live in filth, but he also didn't appreciate her diligent efforts to keep their home nice. Instead, he would point out what was wrong . . . with everything, including Abby herself. Nate even picked out Abby's clothes for her. He was incredibly particular about what she was to wear, especially if they were going to go out in public. She certainly wasn't allowed to wear revealing clothes. All her skirts had to hit below the knees.

Plus, she was forced to take a shower every day. Admittedly, Abby wouldn't have disagreed with this in general, but she was only allowed to take a ten-minute shower. Nate literally timed her. If Abby went over the time limit, he would just shut the water off on her. Then, when she got out of the bathroom, Nate would shout that he was the one working and making the money. He was the one who paid the bills.

Abby was used to the yelling. No matter how hard she worked to ensure everything she did met Nate's expectations, she was never good enough. Of course, Nate had never been physically abusive to Abby, but that didn't say much. She thought he liked the emotional and psychological torture method better. Plus, people would be able to see the signs of physical violence whereas his preferred form of abuse was invisible.

Fortunately for Nate, Abby was good at hiding the emotional abuse. She made sure that when they were in public, always together, she looked at her husband in a doting way. Of course, Nate would pay attention to her then too. He'd buy her ice cream at the local diner and hold her hand while they walked down the street. However, people didn't notice that he was gripping her hand so tight she was silently flinching in pain. Nate knew that if she got the opportunity, she would run. That's why he never gave her the opportunity. She was his . . . forever.

One day early in their marriage, Abby had been next door at the neighbor's house, having tea on their porch. They'd been having such an enjoyable evening that she had lost track of the time. When she saw Nate's pickup truck pulling into the drive, she suddenly realized that dinner wasn't ready for him, and he was bound to be furious.

That was the last time she'd sat on her neighbor's porch. Nate made sure that she never ventured outside the house again without him. When he left for work, he would lock the house from the outside. He hid it very well; even the postman didn't see the locks when he left the mail on the porch box every day. Abby knew better than to call out for help when he or anyone else showed up on the doorstep. Nate would be very angry if she disobeyed him, and she didn't want to make him angry.

As long as Abby followed his rules, he was at least kinder to her. After a few years of this behavior, being locked in the house day in and day out, Abby began to ask for small things. She knew that she needed to gain his trust over time, so that's what she did. First, she asked Nate for books—recipe books in particular. She figured if she kept Nate happy, then he wouldn't yell at her as much. From these books, she learned to cook all kinds of good food.

Then, for Christmas one year, Nate got her a tablet. She wasn't really good with technology, but he said she could look up even more recipes online. That's how she'd met

Thomas. Abby had joined a recipe chatroom and started casual conversation with the group. Realizing how much she missed social interaction, she found herself in the chatroom whenever she could.

There was one person whom she especially liked to talk to. Thomas would ask her how her day was while they discussed the amount of salt to add to a casserole. Abby was shy at first and only answered with one-word explanations, but soon, she was eager for Nate to leave for work so she could log on and talk with Thomas, who was only in the chatroom in the mornings and evenings. She knew he must have a job, but talking to him just a couple of times per day gave her something to look forward to.

They eventually shared email addresses, and that's really when the online relationship started. Thomas and Abby had never met face to face, but even online, he treated her better than Nate did. Abby eventually told Thomas about Nate and the way he behaved toward her. Thomas was so supportive through it that she would get random emails from him, checking on her and asking her if anything had happened that day.

Despite the risks, Abby had managed to keep this online relationship away from Nate for over a year. Meanwhile, this new relationship started getting more and more serious. Both Abby and Thomas confessed their secret love to each other and began making plans for Abby to leave her miserable marriage. She just had to figure out how to get out of the house.

Thomas lived in West Virginia. If needed, he had agreed to come to Kentucky to pick her up, but Abby didn't want him around Nate. She was afraid of what would happen.

One spring morning, Abby was in the shower. She had gotten smart and taken an alarm clock into the bathroom so she would never go over Nate's ten-minute rule. She had just toweled off and was putting on her clothes when the bathroom door flew open. Nate had her tablet in his hand, and his face was blood red.

Abby knew then that it was over. Her will to live that day and finally escape Nate was what kept her alive—that and the fact that she'd already begun putting an escape plan in place. You see, there was a window in the bathroom. Nate never intruded when Abby was in there. He did give her that private space and (extremely limited) amount of time. So Abby had been slowly cranking the window open over the last month. She brought the alarm clock in with her so she could mask the scraping sounds with the noise of the water while still allowing enough time to swiftly clean herself. Nate didn't even notice.

The window was her escape route. She was planning on leaving during one of her showers, and by the time Nate figured out something was wrong, she would be long gone. She had even practiced getting in and out of the window multiple times and had figured out which way would be the fastest.

Now, Abby was standing face to face with a Nate she had never experienced before. The look of outrage on his face struck genuine fear in Abby's heart. Nate took a step toward her, raised his right hand, and slapped her across the face so hard that Abby saw stars. That was all it took for her to gain the courage she needed. She may have been emotionally and psychologically tortured for years, locked in her own house and treated like a slave instead of a wife, but she was not going to stay around and let Nate treat her like a punching bag.

"I hope you realize you're never going to leave me," Nate snarled as he turned away from her and launched the tablet through the air. It hit the kitchen wall and shattered into a million pieces. Although Abby was sure things would only get worse, Nate started to retreat.

Just as Nate turned the corner, moving out of Abby's sight, she whirled around and slid the window up without a sound. She had no shoes and only the clothes she was wearing, but that was enough for her. With a stronger resolve than she'd ever experienced, she silently lifted herself onto the window sill and slipped through. The grass under the window was still soft and cool with dew. Barely registering the chill on the soles of her feet, Abby hightailed it across the lawn to her car. Luckily, the keys were still in the ignition, just as she expected. People living in small towns in Kentucky didn't lock their doors or remove their keys from their vehicles. Everyone knew everyone, and if something was afoot, the entire town would know about it before the local cops did.

Abby slid into the vehicle and grasped the steering wheel with trembling hands. It had been a while since she'd driven a car. Nate never allowed her to. With a strange sense of empowerment, Abby turned the key in the switch, and the car rumbled to life. After putting the car in drive, she pressed her bare foot down on the accelerator. The vehicle immediately jumped to life and began following the gravel driveway. Glancing in the rearview mirror, she saw the front door swing open. Nate stepped out onto the porch but went no further. Abby knew he didn't love her. He loved his control over her, and he had just lost it.

Abby let out a long-held breath and smiled. She had beaten Nate at his own game. *She was free.*

CHAPTER
10

The chief found Raelynn in her office bright and early. Forgoing a typical greeting, he walked in, sat down across from her, and handed her a cup of coffee. "I saw the coffee shop was closed this morning, so I figured you might need this."

Raelynn accepted the proffered coffee with a gracious smile. She had checked her email first thing that morning, but to her dismay, there wasn't anything from the county clerk or Darla yet.

"Get any answers yesterday?" The chief inquired.

"I only made it to the coffee shop. Mickey didn't know much. He just said that Kate seemed more preoccupied with her phone recently. I figure I'll see if her parents have her cell phone since we didn't find it at the crime scene."

Raelynn knew this was a long shot. Who would leave their cell phone at home when they were supposed to go on vacation? Kate was still living with her parents, which was not unusual for this neck of the woods. Since Kate had decided not to go to college, her parents had told her they would help her find her own place once she'd saved up some money. That had been a couple of years ago. It seemed that Kate was unable to squirrel away enough money, or maybe she just liked living rent free with her parents. Who wouldn't?

"I thought I would wait around until Monte gets in with the crime scene photos before I start with interviews this morning," Raelynn stated. The chief had asked Monte to assist her with the investigation, so he was working split shifts for a bit. Perhaps it was unrealistic, but she was hoping something in a picture would jump out at her.

At precisely that moment, as if he knew Raelynn and the chief were talking about him, Monte walked in carrying a manila envelope.

"Well, that turned into a disaster," Monte opened with. "These are the crime scene photos and Darla's pictures of the medical exam. Apparently, the photo clerk knew Kate. You can imagine, she started bawling when the pictures began printing out."

"How'd you handle that?" Chief asked.

"At first, I let her cry. You know, get it out of her system. Then, I saw an opportunity since she knew Kate. I asked questions." He looked at the chief and shrugged. The cop had come out in him obviously.

"You never were the most sympathetic person," Chief agreed, shaking his head. "The real question is . . . did you find out anything?"

"Well, maybe," answered Monte. "Although the photo clerk and Kate haven't talked in years, she was able to give me some background on her. It seems that even though Kate may not have been interested in anyone romantically right now, that was not the case in high school."

Raelynn motioned for Monte to take the other empty chair in her office and, with a flick of her hand, invited him to continue his story.

"So Kate apparently had a huge attraction to a certain individual in high school. It was rumored that this crush turned into something more."

Raelynn knew this could just be high school gossip at its best, but Monte still had her on the edge of her seat. "You mean Adam? We already know this and what happened." Raelynn figured this was a dead end.

"It wasn't just Adam that Kate was interested in," he replied. Raelynn turned and exchanged an exasperated look with the chief. Monte sure could keep an audience trailing on after his stories.

"Well, who was it?" The chief was just as curious as she was.

"It was Thomas Ball," Monte stated with an air of someone breaking major news.

"The history teacher?" Raelynn inquired, raising her eyebrows slightly.

"Not only the history teacher but also the track coach," Monte clarified.

Raelynn took a minute to process this new information. If she remembered correctly, Kate never ran track, and Mr. Ball taught advanced college prep classes. She wondered what the connection was.

"So what happened? How'd it start?" Raelynn needed to know more. She began running scenarios through her head. Could Mr. Ball be a suspect? She would definitely put him on her person of interest list, which was pretty darn short at the moment. Actually, he was already at the top.

"Well, rumor has it that Kate started showing up at track practices and meets. Mr. Ball would end up giving her a lift home, and the relationship progressed from there. The photo chick said that Kate got really obsessed with him and wanted to get married, but Mr. Ball started backing away. She said Kate took it hard and started failing classes because she stopped coming to school. After graduation, it just ended," Monte explained.

"Mr. Ball still teaches over at the high school, correct?" the chief asked.

As far as Raelynn knew, he did. Once you got a job around here, you typically didn't find another one.

Raelynn's mind began to theorize what could have occurred between Thomas and Kate. *Maybe he was just a mentor to her? Surely, he wouldn't be stupid enough to get into a situation that could get him arrested.* He seemed like a decent enough guy to her, but who knew what people were really like behind closed doors?

By Raelynn's standards, Mr. Ball would fall into the category of good-looking. Since he was a track coach, Mr. Ball was in good physical shape. In fact, Raelynn would consider him a Mark Wahlberg with glasses.

"I'll make a trip over to the school at the end of the day," Raelynn pronounced. "I want to go see Kate's parents this morning. I also want to interview some of Kate's coworkers. They may be able to provide more information than Mickey did."

As the chief and Monte got up to leave, Raelynn picked up the manila envelope containing the pictures. Before opening it, she took a long drink of coffee and instantly grimaced. Station java definitely didn't compare to that from the coffee shop. It was so strong, it would stand up on its own, but Raelynn believed today would be a day for lots of coffee, no matter the quality, with all the interviews she was going to conduct. Finally, Raelynn opened the manila envelope and exhaled slowly, trying to mentally prepare herself to see the crime scene again.

Monte was good at taking photos. His years of experience on the force helped him pay attention to detail. The pictures started with an overview of the general area and slowly crept closer to the body. To stay organized, Raelynn laid the pictures out on her desk. She was trying to comprehend where each piece of evidence was in relation to Kate's body, sort of like putting a puzzle together. Honestly, there hadn't been a whole lot of evidence found at the crime scene. One of the rose petals had either fallen or been blown out of Kate's hand and was lying beside her. Then, there was the broken tree limb. Wait . . . Raelynn scanned through the pictures but couldn't find the one of the tree limb. How could Monte miss that? She had even talked to him about people who lived nearby.

Shaking her head in frustration, Raelynn picked up a picture of Kate's body and concentrated on the red lingerie. It looked like it was a perfect fit. That was unusual. When perpetrators dressed their victims, most of the time, the clothes didn't fit properly. That was because perpetrators typically didn't really know their victims beforehand and had to guess their sizes. This was not the case with Kate.

Nothing stood out in particular about the lingerie—although Raelynn had to admit she was not an expert in this area. She had never bought anything like this, let alone worn it. The lingerie was a one-piece garment that flowed loosely around the body. Raelynn thought the term "babydoll" came to mind. There was a little bit of lace around the top. *Hmm.*

So far, everything indicated that Kate had known her perpetrator. Maybe Kate had taken some time off work to have a good time with a guy friend? But how did she end up on the Seneca Creek Trail? What had happened in the meantime?

Raelynn didn't find any answers in the photos after her initial look. She rose from her seat, hoping her interviews that day would shed more light on the situation. But until then, there was coffee. She grimaced again as she took a final sip.

CHAPTER
11

Abby saw the red and blue lights and knew they were for her. She had been speeding all night. She just wanted to get as far away as she could as fast as she could. She guessed she was going a bit too fast. She had crossed over the West Virginia border about half an hour previously, but she hadn't let up. She knew she was a target because she had out-of-state tags. Add the speeding, and it wasn't surprising the red and blue lights were coming after her.

As Abby pulled to the side of the road, she glanced in the rearview mirror. She definitely looked like a hot mess. Her face was turning from red to black where Nate had hit her, and she didn't have on shoes. Luckily, Abby's purse was tucked away in the middle console of the car. The last time they had gone to town, she'd made sure to leave it in there purely as a piece in her escape plan.

As if she hadn't been through enough for today, now she had to deal with a cop. Abby took a few deep breaths, trying to calm herself down.

It seemed like an eternity passed before the cop came into view. Or, at least, she assumed it was a cop. He wasn't dressed in the typical patrolman uniform.

Abby rolled the driver's side window down but didn't turn her head toward the officer. She didn't want him to see her face and was hoping her long brunette hair would hide it.

"Hello, ma'am. May I see your license and insurance?" the officer asked. Nodding vaguely, Abby reached into the middle console and retrieved her purse. There wasn't much else in there other than her wallet. She handed the officer her driver's license, still without glancing his way.

"Thank you. I'll be back in a sec." Abby watched the cop walk back to his cruiser, appearing fit and confident. She sat in silence for what seemed like a decade until the officer returned to her car.

"Here's your operators back and a warning ticket. How come you were driving so fast back there?" the officer asked. Abby looked down at her lap. She hadn't thought about how to answer the officer's questions. Out of a nervous habit, Abby tucked her hair behind her ears, momentarily forgetting about the bruise that was developing on the side of her face.

"Oh, Ms. Jones, are you okay?" Of course, the officer saw the bruise. Abby turned her head in the direction of the officer's voice. It was at this moment, when he expressed concern for her, that Abby emotionally broke down. She could feel the tears begin to flow as the floodgates opened. She tried to regain composure, wiping the tears from her face. The officer didn't say anything, just let her weep.

"I'm so sorry. I didn't mean to cry," Abby stammered. "It's just been a rough day."

"Do you want to talk about it?" the officer asked. Abby stared at him. *Does he really care or is this part of his job?* Abby didn't know what it was about the officer, but she spilled her guts out to him. She told him everything about Nate, but she didn't tell him why he'd gotten so upset with her. She just said the abuse had finally turned physical, so she'd left. Showing great compassion, the officer didn't interrupt her as she told her story. By the end, Abby had cried all the tears that she had kept stored up after years of abuse.

"So what's your plan now? Do you have some place to go?" the officer asked. Abby really hadn't thought about where she was going. She hadn't been able to contact Thomas since she had left. He'd probably been sending her emails and wondering why she hadn't replied. She knew he'd be worried. When she'd gotten in her car, she'd just driven to West Virginia. Unfortunately, she didn't even know where Thomas lived. Now that the officer was asking her these questions, she realized she didn't know what her plan was.

Abby shook her head no, fighting the fresh tears that were threatening to fall again. She felt lost. "I figured I could find a hotel or something."

The officer chuckled at that. "There are no hotels around here anywhere close, but I may know of a place where you can stay," he offered. "Why don't you follow me?"

Abby didn't have many options right now. She was alone and didn't know how to get in touch with Thomas. This officer was lending a hand and trying to give her help. She had nowhere else to turn. So Abby put her car in drive and pulled out behind the officer's cruiser. She tried to keep faith that her life would get better after today. At least she had one person on her side.

CHAPTER
12

Raelynn sauntered into Seneca Rocks High School just as the buses were pulling out for evening drop-off. The smell of lockers and sweat filled her sinuses and brought back memories from the days she'd attended. Raelynn's last year of high school had seemed to drag on after she lost her mom. Everything she'd experienced, such as prom and graduation, seemed like a waste without her mother being there to experience it with her. Gulping back a wave of sadness, Raelynn shook her head and forced the memories to subside.

It had already been a rough day. She'd just come from Mr. and Mrs. Williams' home, where she'd introduced herself and gently prodded them for information about Kate. Unfortunately, she'd walked away without any new insights at all. Kate's mother had tearfully exclaimed that she couldn't imagine who would do such a thing to her baby after all she'd been through already. Kate's father had stood stiffly in silence until, as a fresh wave of grief overtook Mrs. Williams, he'd strode forward and asked Raelynn to leave, insisting they had nothing of value to contribute to the investigation. She'd made a hasty exit at that point, but she couldn't forget that last image of husband and wife holding each other, shoulders shaking, both broken and looking to each other for some form of solace.

Within moments, she found herself standing in the receptionist's office, where she asked to see Mr. Ball. The receptionist was the same lady as when Raelynn had attended high school. She had been old then, and she hadn't changed one bit—same white hair fashioned into a beehive from the seventies.

Feeling antsy, Raelynn decided to step out into the hall to wait. A few minutes later, she spotted him making his way down the hallway toward her. She took this time to get a good look at Mr. Ball. She could understand why students would be attracted to him. He had the tall, dark, and handsome vibe. By her estimate, he was in his early thirties. Dressed neatly in khaki slacks and a polo, he was fit and had a slight air of confidence that wafted from him.

Raelynn took a couple of steps forward with an outstretched hand. "Mr. Ball, I'm Detective Bailey. Do you have a moment?"

After briefly but firmly shaking her hand, Mr. Ball replied, "Sure. Let's go in this empty classroom."

As Raelynn entered the room full of desks and textbooks, she fought the years of memories coming back. Her high school years were definitely a period that she didn't want to revisit. It wasn't like she'd had a horrible high school experience; it was just that she hadn't had a great experience either. Most of the time, she'd fit in with her classmates but felt like a loner.

Shaking off the unwelcome recollections of her adolescence, Raelynn slid into one of the desks across from Mr. Ball, although the task wasn't easy with her gun attached to her side. She seemed to realize that these desks were not adapted to fit someone of her size and age. Glancing down, she noted the initials of what seemed like hundreds of students who had sat in this same seat. Undoubtedly, the underside of the desk housed wads of hardened chewing gum discarded by students busted by the teacher.

Mr. Ball leaned back in his chair, trying to come across as relaxed, though there was a tinge of concern in his expression. "What can I help you with, Detective?"

Raelynn decided to get directly to the point. "I'm here regarding a former student of yours. Katherine Williams. She went by Kate." She introduced the victim in this particular manner so she could gauge Mr. Ball's reaction to her name.

Although it had been three years since Kate had graduated, his reaction to her name definitely conveyed recognition. He nodded his head, acknowledging his familiarity with the young woman. "I remember Kate. I didn't have her in class, but I remember her in general."

Raelynn sat back and tried not to smile at his response. Without vocalizing a reply, she waited expectantly for Mr. Ball to continue.

"I teach advanced classes to prepare students for college. You know, like calculus and trigonometry. Kate never signed up for those types of classes."

"How well did you know Kate, Mr. Ball?"

"I'm not sure I really understand your question," he countered, a frown creasing his forehead. "I mean, I knew her from passing in the halls and such but not much more than any other student."

Raelynn took a moment to let his answer sink in. She noticed that he was fidgeting in his seat, and a small bead of sweat appeared on his forehead. *Hmm, someone's lying.*

"Let me be clear, Mr. Ball," Raelynn said in a low, serious voice, leaning forward with her elbows on the desk in front of her. "When I ask questions, I usually know the answer already—at least to some extent. So let me ask you again. How well did you know Kate?" She'd hit a nerve this time. Mr. Ball rose from his seat and wandered over to the window. Letting him take his time, Raelynn remained silent, hoping Mr. Ball was gearing up to make a confession.

Finally, Mr. Ball slowly turned his back to the window and crossed his arms. "You know, when I started teaching, I said I would never be one of those teachers."

"What kind of teacher?" Raelynn persisted.

"The kind to fall for a student," Mr. Ball stated as he turned away from Raelynn again. "Like I said, I never taught Kate in class. That part is true. I don't know if you know this, but I coach the girls' track team. Kate started showing up at the practices. She would just sit on the bleachers and watch. I thought she wanted to be part of the team or was there supporting a friend. One evening, I walked over to her and asked." Mr. Ball suddenly let out a chuckle. "Sorry, I'm just thinking back on that day. I mean, you know Kate. She definitely isn't subtle. Whatever was on her mind, she said."

Raelynn nodded in agreement and reluctantly allowed the right side of her mouth to quirk up in a half smile. That was certainly true about Kate.

"Anyway, I walked over, introduced myself to her, and asked if she was interested in joining the team. Kate just smiled and said she wasn't interested in the team—she was interested in me. Point blank. To the point. That was Kate, and I instantly liked her. She kept coming to the practices and even to the track meets. It really didn't even start out as anything other than friendship. I would drive her home, and we would just talk."

Mr. Ball sat back down across from Raelynn but had a hard time looking her in the eye. Raelynn could tell he had feelings for Kate—that this was hard to talk about. Of course, he probably hadn't heard that she was dead yet. If he had, he was hiding it quite well.

"Do you remember when this started?" Raelynn asked.

"Well, track season starts in March and goes until the end of the school year. I believe it was her senior year," he guessed.

"Tell me more." Raelynn was interested in his version of the event compared to that of the circulating rumor.

"I honestly thought at the end of the school year, it would stop. I figured when she wasn't around me, she would just forget about me."

"But that didn't happen, did it?" Raelynn asked.

"No, it actually got worse. Kate figured out where I lived. Of course, that's not hard. There's not that many places to rent around here, and I didn't want to buy a house as a bachelor. So when I heard the apartment above Cooper's Store was available, I jumped on it. It was easy for Kate to come see me. She just told everyone she was going to the store, and instead, she would knock on my door. Eventually, the relationship turned physical. But I swear, it was Kate that started it!"

Ah, here comes the blame, she thought to herself, repressing the urge to roll her eyes. It couldn't be Mr. Ball's fault the relationship had turned physical. It was all Kate's. That was a line that Raelynn had heard a hundred times before.

"So you're telling me that Kate was the aggressor in the relationship? Yet you did nothing to stop it, even though you knew it was wrong." Raelynn's voice was flat.

"Yes, you're completely right," he responded, looking ashamed. "Kate started it, but I didn't stop it. I guess I just figured it would never get to the point it did. That's why I put a stop to it later."

"Tell me what happened."

"It was the end of the summer before school started back up. Kate had just turned nineteen. I sent her roses for her birthday, but she got tremendously upset. I guess she'd thought I was going to propose marriage to her on her birthday. She kept pushing to get married, but there was no way I wanted to do that. So I told her I wanted to end the relationship. She went berserk. She would text me every hour, telling me that we could work it out, telling me how much she loved me. It got so bad I had to change my number." At this point, Mr. Ball's voice had become muffled and faint, as he sat with his head in his hands.

Raelynn was unmoved and plunged forward with her questioning. "So what happened once school started back up?"

"Honestly, I didn't see Kate much. I went back to teaching and coaching just like before. I heard that she decided not to go on to college and got a job at the coffee shop. I guess the breakup really did affect her. Don't think I'm stupid. I heard the rumors. There were so many. The big one was that Kate was knocked up. That one wasn't true. I was very careful with Kate, especially since she told me she was a virgin."

"Have you talked to Kate since she graduated, Mr. Ball?" Raelynn wanted to know if the relationship had picked back up with Kate legally.

"Even though it's a small town, I made it a point not to see her. When I heard she was working at the coffee shop, I made sure to not go near the place."

Raelynn's eyebrows rose. "So you're keeping tabs on her?"

"Like I said, I made it a point not to run into her." Mr. Ball took the offensive. "I moved out of the apartment to clear across town. I also have been dating someone for two years now."

Well, now seemed an appropriate time to start asking the tough questions. Mr. Ball's demeanor had changed from a puppy in love to a territorial chihuahua. "Mr. Ball, where were you Saturday?"

"I was with my girlfriend all weekend. Why?" It seemed a lightbulb had come on over Mr. Ball's head. "What's going on? Why are you really here, Detective?"

"We found Kate's body yesterday morning, Mr. Ball," Raelynn stated bluntly. She provided no other information. With all her senses perked up, she simply sat there witnessing Mr. Ball's reaction to the news. To her surprise, the territorial chihuahua promptly turned into a blubbering idiot. Struck dumb with devastation, Mr. Ball couldn't even form sentences. He covered his face with his hands and openly wept. Raelynn could guess the reaction was genuine. He truly loved her, no matter how wrong it had been.

Raelynn gave him a few minutes to attempt composure. Finally, Mr. Ball fell into silence and stared at her with a look of numb disbelief.

"Do you know anyone that Kate was seeing lately?" Raelynn knew this was a longshot but had to ask.

Mr. Ball continued sitting in silence for a moment before responding. "Why would I know that?"

"Well, Mr. Ball, you are the only living person we know she had a relationship with. Typically, when a relationship ends sort of nasty like yours did, some kind of revenge could be involved," Raelynn pointed out. "And you said you were keeping tabs on her."

"Wait, you think I killed Kate because she was seeing someone else? I told you I keep away from her. And I wouldn't do that anyway. I didn't care who Kate saw. I am in my own relationship now." There was a clear ring of defensiveness in Mr. Ball's tone at this point. Frankly, Raelynn couldn't blame him. She'd just made him admit to having an affair with a student, and now she'd told him that student was dead. Still, she had a job to do. She couldn't waste time being gentle with people who were viable suspects in a potential homicide.

"So you're telling me that this is the first time you have heard about Kate? No one mentioned it to you before now?"

"No, this is the first time. I came right into the school this morning and started teaching." He paused a moment, thinking quietly. Then, he continued. "Well, I guess there could have been talk about it, but I don't hang around with the other staff too much."

"This morning . . . But what about yesterday? You didn't hear anything then?" Raelynn inquired.

"No, I was with my girlfriend. We went away for a long weekend. I didn't come back to work until today." He was speaking in a steady tone, but his demeanor told her he wasn't telling the truth. Mr. Ball never looked directly at her as he answered her question. In her experience, that was one of the key indicators that someone was lying.

"Right—you mentioned your new girlfriend before. Who is she, and where does she live?"

"Her name is Abby Jones. She's not from around here," Mr. Ball replied in an oddly hesitant voice. "I was with her all weekend. I usually spend my weekends with her."

Raelynn wasn't familiar with Abby Jones. She'd have to contact Ms. Jones to confirm his alibi once she learned more information.

"Look, Mr. Ball, I'm just trying to figure out what happened to Kate. I'm sorry to be bringing you obviously upsetting news. I'll let you get on with your day."

Mr. Ball grunted in acknowledgment. So much for keeping a good rapport with him. Sensing the conversation was drawing to a close, Raelynn stood and turned toward the door, but one final question entered her mind before she could leave.

"Actually, I have one more question. What kind of roses did you give Kate?" Raelynn never told him how Kate's body had been found.

"I don't know how that could possibly relate to Kate's death, but . . . I gave her red ones. Red was Kate's favorite color. She wore it almost every day."

At that point, Mr. Ball looked away from Raelynn, signifying that was the end of the discussion. Recognizing he was done talking, she turned and headed out of the school.

So red was Kate's favorite color. And it was the color of the nightie she'd been found wearing. What were the chances that was a coincidence?

CHAPTER
13

The house that she was staying in was quaint. There wasn't much furniture, but she didn't have anything to her name, so it seemed fitting. When she awoke the next morning, she knew she needed to find Thomas. And since she'd recovered from her hysterical crying, she wanted to find the officer who'd helped her out and thank him.

First stop in her new life: find a phone and get some shoes. Abby visited the local convenience store, hoping they would have what she needed. Luckily, she found a Tracfone with rechargeable minutes. They didn't have much in the way of shoes, but she plucked up a pair of flip-flops that would do until she could find something else.

The first thing she did after powering on her phone was send Thomas an email. Hopefully, the lack of communication hadn't pushed him away. She really needed his support right now. Since Abby didn't know where Thomas lived, she simply gave him her current address in hopes he would stop by.

As she meandered down the street, Abby spied a coffee shop, and her tummy told her she needed some caffeine fuel for the day. So she opened the door and bravely entered, the heavenly smell of coffee filling her senses. After glancing around and noting the few other patrons minding their own business, Abby sat down at the counter.

Almost immediately, a man with blue hair walked through the door behind the counter, a grin illuminating his face. "Welcome to The Roast. What can I get ya?"

Abby smiled. There was something about the man's personality that brightened her day. Not to mention his hair matched his shirt. "Well, I'm not sure. What's good here?"

Apparently, the man found her question funny. He chuckled but replied, "In my opinion, everything is good here."

Smiling at his witty response, Abby ultimately ordered the special coffee of the day and a bagel with extra cream cheese. Then, she sat contently eating her breakfast and people watching. It was time to begin her new life—and it felt better than she could have ever imagined.

CHAPTER
14

Raelynn rolled over in bed and looked at the alarm clock. She could never sleep past six-thirty in the morning. Today was the same, of course. She hadn't expected anything different, especially since she was dreading what the day would bring.

Today was Kate's funeral. Still groggy from sleep, Raelynn set about trying to mentally prepare to see her family. In an effort to be sensitive to their needs, she was waiting until after the funeral to talk to them again. She figured she would give them time to mourn.

With a wide yawn and a crack of her neck, Raelynn flipped back the covers and swung her legs out of bed. At least last night she hadn't had the nightmare, but she also hadn't drunk a beer before going to bed. Was that the trick? Her mom had always told her to drink milk before going to sleep because it helped with the dreams. Maybe it was time to try that.

Still stretching and rolling her shoulders, Raelynn walked to the closet, once again pondering what to wear. Luckily, it was a pretty easy choice this time, at least on the surface. She immediately pulled out her one and only black dress—the one she hadn't worn since her father's funeral.

She hated going to the funeral home. Why get dressed up in something to mourn the dead? They couldn't see what you had on. They didn't care. They were *gone*. With that thought, she put the dress back. She would just sort of fancy up her daily attire. Besides, she was still working today.

In the end, she decided on a black and white striped shirt with black dress pants. For extra measure, she grabbed her suit jacket that she normally wore to court. *There*. That would do.

The viewing would go from nine until twelve o'clock, at which point everyone would head to the cemetery for the burial. The whole town was expected to show for the visitation at least. That's how popular Kate was. Raelynn planned on being there at least most of the day. She wanted to see who attended and was determined to note whether anyone acted strange or looked out of place.

Raelynn knew the coffee shop would be closed out of respect for Kate. Without the support of her daily cappuccino, Raelynn took some extra time to brew a pot of coffee. There was no way she was going to rely on the station's subpar variant. That was like drinking turpentine. With practiced motions, Raelynn prepared a large thermos and grabbed her car keys.

Raelynn pulled into the parking lot of the local funeral home. It was early, and there wasn't a lot of traffic yet. After debating for a moment on where to park, she chose a spot that provided a clear view of the front door. Unless she saw something or someone she thought was important, she wouldn't leave the confines of her cruiser. She was just planning on camping out and keeping watch. Perhaps the culprit would want to attend Kate's viewing but would be too nervous to actually enter the building. Raelynn would keep an eagle eye to notice anything like that. Meanwhile, Dane and Tony were already inside the funeral home, presumably watching everyone in the vicinity.

Two hours into the stakeout, Raelynn realized her cruiser was not very comfortable. Plus, she had drunk all her coffee and needed to find a bathroom. So she opened the car door and was about to go inside when she spotted a familiar face. Mr. Ball was getting out of a Jeep across the parking lot, clearly about to enter the funeral home. Ducking her head, Raelynn decided to take her time and slip in behind him.

She found it interesting that he'd come by himself. Although his girlfriend may not have known Kate, Raelynn knew significant others would typically show up for emotional support. Maybe Mr. Ball didn't want Abby to know that he was coming to the funeral home. Or maybe he'd told her he was going simply because Kate used to be his student.

Still being as discreet as possible, Raelynn slid into the back row of the funeral home's main parlor after nodding surreptitiously at Tony, who was lolling against the back wall. As was typical for a town of this size, this was the only funeral home, owned and operated by the same family as when her parents had died. The quietly impressive building was a large historic mansion-style house that was hemmed in by a large wraparound porch. White board siding and black shutters gave the business a feeling of austere calm. The flower boxes on the porch were just now getting an early batch of flowers put in, providing a dollop of color and cheer despite the sad circumstances that brought visitors every day.

Inside, each room was designated for specific purposes. The large main parlor was used for viewing and services. Then, there were two additional rooms that flanked the parlor. One was set up as an escape for family in case events became overwhelming. The other was used to provide refreshments. Bathrooms were located down a hallway that led to offices, and a display of caskets was housed in a garage around the back. The owners still lived on site, taking up the entire second floor. Finally, the basement of the mansion provided the embalming services.

The main parlor sitting area was arranged to accommodate the largest crowd possible. Rows and rows of folding chairs had been erected with enough space to create a pathway around the outer perimeter so grieving parties could come and go with ease. There were several people among the chairs, most talking tensely and looking around suspiciously as they speculated what could have happened to this young girl who had died far too soon.

Kate's casket was front and center. Large flower arrangements adorned each side, finding solemn company with various other items, such as lanterns, memorial blankets, and windchimes.

Raelynn watched with anticipation as Mr. Ball approached the casket and awaiting family members. Surely, Kate's family had heard the rumors about the two of them. Mr. Ball stopped at the casket and took a long look at Kate. As he turned toward her parents, Raelynn could see he was openly crying. There was no doubt he still had feelings for Kate, even though he'd said he made it a point to not run into her. After quickly walking through the line leading up to Kate's parents, he shook their hands and expressed his condolences. They didn't seem to mind him being there. Maybe they were unaware of his involvement with Kate. Raelynn supposed she would find out soon enough.

Raelynn thought she was being fairly unobtrusive, but Mr. Ball caught her eye as he walked out of the funeral home. He nodded and left without a word. Suddenly remembering why she had entered the funeral home in the first place, Raelynn glanced around, this time at doorways rather than at people. She needed to find a bathroom.

After relieving herself, Raelynn decided to go ahead and make an appearance for Kate's family before heading back to the parking lot. With an appropriately somber look on her face, she approached the viewing line. There had been a steady procession of people coming to pay their respects, but no one stood out to Raelynn other than Mr. Ball and Dane, who hesitated briefly in front of Kate's casket and stuttered out an apology to her parents before stalking away, hands deep in his uniform pockets.

Raelynn took a deep, calming breath to center herself as she reached the front of the line. "Mr. and Mrs. Williams. Again, I'm so sorry for your loss. I can't imagine how difficult this must be for you."

"Thank you, Detective. Just find out what happened to our baby girl," Mr. Williams whispered in a broken voice as Raelynn shook their hands.

She didn't dare make promises she couldn't necessarily keep, but she gave them a halfhearted nod and said, "I'll be in touch." Then, Raelynn turned on her heel and went back to her cruiser. Although she'd planned to stick around for the entirety of the day, she decided she'd changed her mind. Dane and Tony had things covered inside, and what were the chances that someone would be hanging around the outside of the funeral home anyway? She figured she could put her day to better use.

After grabbing a quick lunch at the diner, Raelynn marched into the squad room. The patrol officers were out of the office, and the chief had said he wouldn't be in until after he'd paid his respects at the funeral. Since Raelynn hadn't seen him, she assumed he hadn't made it over there yet.

Actually, Raelynn thought it was unusual for the chief not to come into work first. Come to think of it, she had noticed over the past month or so that he would randomly leave before his shift was over. Technically, he didn't have a shift, but everyone knew that he worked during the day. As of late, Raelynn would find him coming in later or taking longer lunches. *Odd.*

The office was nice and quiet, a rare treat that Raelynn enjoyed. Her first move was to check her email. Though it seemed unlikely based on the initial timeframe she'd been given, she was hoping for an email from the county clerk with property information. However, she'd also be happy to receive the test results on Kate's toxicology.

As she waited for her computer to load, Raelynn pulled out the photographs again. As she methodically reviewed them, taking care to scan every piece of every photo, she couldn't help but think there was something she had missed. She just couldn't put her finger on it right now.

Suddenly, Raelynn's email dinged. Yes! She had a new message. Focusing her attention back on her computer, she noted with glee that the toxicology results had arrived. She was one for two.

One of the great things about Darla was that she was always good about providing a narrative with any test results. She understood that laymen had a difficult time interpreting medical lingo. So this email provided a clear explanation of the findings, along with the official toxicology report. However, after skimming through the information, she realized she may have to give Darla a call anyway. Apparently, Kate had a large, and potentially fatal, amount of rocuronium in her body. That was interesting because rocuronium was a paralytic drug used mainly during surgery, according to Darla's email narrative. But what did that mean exactly? Raelynn picked up her phone.

"You got my email, huh?" Darla answered without even a hello. That made Raelynn giggle.

"You know me too well. So give me your opinion."

"I was honestly surprised by the rocuronium. I figured that if she was positive for any drugs, it would be something illegal, like heroin. The good news is the rocuronium gives you some type of path to follow," Darla opined.

"What do you mean by that?" asked Raelynn.

"Well, it's a drug that is definitely only found at a hospital. Not so much at a walk-in clinic. It's typically used to sedate patients before going into surgery. Usually administered by an anesthesiologist, but nursing staff may administer it too. It relaxes a person's muscles, so it is often used before they are intubated," Darla explained.

"So you've narrowed my list of suspects to everyone who works at the hospital essentially." Despite the promise this lead offered, Raelynn was not enthused.

"Well, if you look at it that way, I guess so. Sorry," Darla answered with little sympathy.

Her mind jumbled up with these new details, Raelynn thanked Darla for the information and let her go. At least it was reassuring that Kate didn't have illegal substances in her system. However, Raelynn believed it was time to officially call Kate's death a homicide. She definitely wouldn't have injected herself with rocuronium unless she thought it was something else.

The theories kept mounting in Raelynn's overloaded brain. One such theory was that Kate had been in a consensual relationship with a male whom she didn't want anyone to know about. If she could believe Mr. Ball, which Raelynn was still on the fence about, maybe Kate had gotten emotionally attached to a new guy. Perhaps this had caused him to kill her, and maybe the killer had wanted to embarrass Kate by dressing her in red lingerie. Maybe he'd wanted to expose her "true" nature.

Of course, there were also the red roses. What were those all about? Raelynn was stuck on the fact that Mr. Ball knew what her favorite color was and then it miraculously showed up at the crime scene. Clearly, Raelynn needed to follow up with Mr. Ball's girlfriend to confirm his alibi. Until then, he'd remain at the top of the suspect list. Admittedly, she wasn't sure how he would get access to the drug, but she would figure that out later.

CHAPTER
15

Earlier, at the coffee shop, the owner had mentioned the best place to grab a meal was the diner up the street. That had piqued Abby's interest, and she decided to try it out. Abby took a seat at a back table in the local diner. She quickly found that the food here was good and consisted of true home cooking.

On her way to the table, Abby had picked up a local tourist guide that had been abandoned on a nearby chair and flipped the pages. If she was going to stay here for any length of time, she needed to gather knowledge of her surroundings. The cell phone that she'd bought was laying face up on the table. Abby kept checking it every few minutes, even though she knew it was unlikely that Thomas would email her back. He was probably in class already.

Abby was so engrossed in the brochure that she didn't even hear the diner's door open, and she certainly didn't pay attention to who had walked through. It wasn't until he was hovering over her table that she realized he was there.

"Mind if I sit?"

Abby looked up when she heard the familiar voice. Unbidden, a huge smile spread across her face. Momentarily speechless at the shock of unexpectedly seeing him again, she nodded her head, and he slid into the booth across from her.

"I was going to try to come find you. I wanted to tell you how grateful I am that you found me a place to stay so quickly," Abby exclaimed when she finally found her voice. As she looked across the table at him, she noted that he emanated a sense of security and sincerity. She hadn't felt that in a long time. Although it was the last thing that should have been on her mind, Abby had to admit he was attractive.

"Well, I'm just glad I could help. Any idea what your next steps are at this point?"

Abby shook her head and took a sip of her coffee before holding up the town brochure. "This place doesn't seem too bad," she replied with a half grin.

He chuckled, and she noticed his laugh was deep and throaty. "Take as much time as you need. The place you're staying at isn't going anywhere for a while," he replied. "You could even get a job around here. Mickey's always looking for help." He smiled, eyes glinting. "Maybe I'll swing by later today and see if you need anything, but right now, I have to head out," he commented.

"That would be very nice. Thank you," she responded almost coyly.

As she watched him get up from the booth and strut toward the door, she found herself hoping he *would* stop by her makeshift home. She really wanted him to. *Get a grip*, she thought to herself, trying not to bestow too much gratitude upon him. He was probably just feeling pity for her and her situation, but she secretly hoped there might be something more. *But why would you care about that? You have Thomas!* She really had to get her unruly thoughts under control.

Abby allowed herself to truly savor her meal. She really liked this place, and so far, she was really liking this town. But before she could sink too far into her daydream about her new future, she wondered what Nate was doing. Was he pacing the house, worrying about her? Was he out looking for her, desperate to get her back? Had he realized he truly did love her after all and wanted to change to keep their marriage intact?

Then, she found herself thinking about Thomas. Abby didn't consider herself to be a particularly pretty girl. She certainly didn't stick out in crowds because of her good looks, and she never kept up with beauty or fashion trends. So she wasn't used to the attention that Thomas had given her over the past two years. He was so reassuring—the only person she'd confided in about how Nate treated her. She knew that she had fallen in love with him, even though she hadn't met him face to face yet. On the flip side, even though Nate had treated her badly, she still had feelings for him too. He was her first love.

Abby huffed out a frustrated sigh, unable to understand this struggle with her feelings. But she had a plan. Once she saw Thomas, she would know the true answer in her heart. In the meantime, she was torn.

Abby didn't realize she was in such a trance until she heard a light tap on the table. She startled at the sound.

"Sorry, I didn't mean to scare you," apologized the man with blue hair from the coffee shop. "I was just checking to make sure you were alright. You seemed spaced out for a bit there."

"Oh, yes. Sorry. I guess I was in my own little world," Abby muttered as a shy smile crossed her face. The man slid in the booth across from her. She hadn't expected to entertain company while she consumed the rest of her lunch, and now this was the second guy who had sat down across from her. Unsure what to do, Abby picked up her coffee again and sat back into the booth. She didn't like having this much attention on her.

"I'm Mickey," the man said, kindly leaning back to give her a bit of space. It seemed he'd noticed her discomfort. "I own the coffee shop. I realized I didn't formally introduce myself when you were in earlier."

"Hi, I'm Abby," she replied, still clutching her beverage.

"Are you new in town?" Mickey inquired. "I've lived here all my life but haven't seen you until this morning when you came by the coffee shop." This made Abby withdraw into herself even more. She wasn't used to talking about herself. Plus, she didn't want people to discover her past. What if they knew Nate and told him where she was? She couldn't take that chance.

"Um, yeah, I haven't been in town very long," she finally answered, her eyes skittering all over the interior of the diner. All the while, Abby was thinking of ways to escape the conversation. Fortunately, Mickey must have sensed that coming to Seneca Rocks was a tense subject because he moved on to the next topic.

"What do you think about the coffee?" he asked, pulling his eyebrows together in a comically hopeful expression. Abby more securely wrapped her hands around her handmade crafted mug and raised it to her lips. Taking a moment to breathe in the deep aroma of the freshly brewed coffee, she drew a long, slow sip, letting it coat her mouth and throat.

"I think yours is much more divine," she sighed with another shy smile. Mickey's answering beam was like none she had seen. There was something about him that was charismatic yet calming.

"I'm glad you liked it. I visited Colombia and was able to warm my palate with some of the best coffee. I knew that I wanted to bring it back with me. That's how the coffee shop started," Mickey explained.

Abby felt entranced by his story. "I heard that you're always looking for help. Are you hiring?" Abby asked, although she had never worked in a coffee shop before. Actually, she'd never had a job other than taking care of the house and cooking for Nate.

To her alarm, Mickey's attitude changed with that question, and Abby realized something was wrong.

"Oh, yeah, I'm looking for a barista," he replied as his gaze slid to look out the window.

Abby let him get lost in thought for a moment before asking, "Are you okay?"

Giving his head a quick shake, Mickey turned back toward her and offered her a half smile.

"Yeah, I'm okay. I just forgot I had a position to fill—that's all." Mickey let out a long breath. "Are you interested?"

"Um, maybe," Abby replied with little confidence. "I don't really know what a barista does. I mean, I probably wouldn't be good at."

Mickey laughed at her response, which made Abby sit up a little straighter as quiet pride stiffened her spine. Was he laughing at her? She was used to that. People had made fun of her a lot in high school. His laugh made her anxious, and she tucked her hair behind her ears out of a nervous habit.

"Sorry, I'm not laughing at you. You aren't the first one around these parts that doesn't know what a barista is," he laughed. "It took folks around here a long time to believe that my coffee is better than what comes out of the at-home coffee pots or this diner's."

"Oh, that makes sense. Where I come from people aren't used to it either," she replied.

"Where's that?" he asked.

"Um." She hesitated again, maybe a moment too long. "Kentucky," she finally answered. She couldn't meet his gaze though. She silently hoped he would let the subject go.

"Well, take your time to think about it," he responded, taking in her mannerisms. Abby was stunned by his response.

"You mean, you would hire me?" she asked. Mickey slid out of the booth and stood up.

"Yeah, there's something about you that I like. You seem like a good person," he replied, then turned and headed to the counter. As she watched him walk away, her hopes for this town rose even higher. This may just be the break she needed to get on with her life.

CHAPTER 16

Abby was sitting on the front porch of her newfound home. She had spent most of the day picking up a few clothing items to get her through the week. All the while, she had compulsively checked her phone for an email from Thomas, but she still hadn't received a response. Could the whole relationship have been in her mind? Did she leave Nate for a man whom she had never met and now may never meet face to face?

Abby liked this place. Seneca Rocks reminded her of Kentucky. There were large mountains and towering trees. Everything was just starting to bud to life. Around the border of the home, Easter lilies and tulips had started to bloom. Abby could smell their sweetness as soon as she stepped out of the house. The serene surroundings were at stark odds with tumult erupting in her mind.

Alone and confused, Abby was thinking about her future. Should she return to Nate? Realistically, this was not a viable option. Nothing good would come of that. Maybe she could start her life here in Seneca Rocks. Was she capable enough to make that happen? She would give herself some time to think things through. In the meantime, Abby was interested in pursuing the job opportunity at the café. The owner, Mickey, apparently liked her, and even though she had never had a job, Abby knew she would be a good fit.

Maybe this was the beginning of a brand-new adventure—one that wouldn't be completely controlled and manipulated by someone who claimed to love her. This was her chance to see what she could accomplish on her own, and while that was certainly intimidating, she also felt oddly liberated by the idea.

A distant rumble caused Abby to glance up. Moments later, a car pulled into the driveway, crunching gravel along the way. A spark of glee shooting up her abdomen, she sat up a little straighter in the porch rocking chair. She had wanted him to show up but had tried not to get her hopes up. Nonetheless, she had made sure to take real good care of the house and look her best just in case.

With a shy smile, Abby watched as he got out of the car and strode her way. Although he was a few years older than her, he was handsome in her eyes. Even better, he was carrying two cups of coffee in his hands. Sighing contentedly, he made himself at home on the porch like he had been there a million times before.

"I took the liberty to get you a coffee from The Roast. I hope that's okay," he stated as he handed her one of the beverages.

Even through the plastic lid, Abby could smell the aroma of freshly brewed coffee. Pleased but a bit awkward, she circled her hands around the cup as a way to calm her nerves. "Wow. First you find me a place to stay, and now you bring me coffee," she replied with a quirk of her lips. Without waiting for his reply, Abby took a sip of the hot latte and let the flavor take over her senses.

"Are you settling in here?" he asked as he lazily rocked in the chair. He must have come over straight after work as he was wearing the same clothes that she had seen him in at the diner.

"I think I'm doing okay. I got a few things to tide me over for about a week. I figured by then I would know if Seneca Rocks is the right place for me," Abby said. She felt so comfortable with him. There didn't seem to be pressure to earn approval when in his presence. Perhaps she was just latching onto anything she could after escaping such a toxic relationship, but she felt like she could be herself around this guy.

"Well, you can stay here as long as you would like. I used to live here years ago and never got rid of it after I moved. Sorry that it seems a little worse for wear. I usually only let friends and relatives stay in it when they are in town."

"Oh, I truly appreciate it. I hadn't really thought of where I was going to stay once I got here. Actually, I hadn't thought much about anything." Abby sort of chuckled and then glanced over at him. He was looking at her intently.

"Feel free to make it your home. I'm sure it could use a woman's touch."

"Thanks," she said, hoping her tone adequately conveyed the true depth of her gratitude. "I'll start paying you back as soon as I get a job and get settled."

"I'm not worried about that. I'm sure we can arrange something," he replied, smiling crookedly at her.

Suddenly, Abby felt a yawn coming on. She figured that the coffee was taking a long time to kick in. And after all, it had been a long day. "I inquired about the job down at the café today," she drawled, blinking heavily.

"That's a great place to work. Mickey is a great guy and really appreciates his employees," he agreed.

Abby was trying to keep up with the conversation, but sleep began to take over. She could faintly hear him talking but couldn't make out the words. She hadn't realized she was so tired. Of course, she had been through a lot over the last two days, so it didn't necessarily surprise her that her body was completely drained. Nearly overcome with exhaustion, Abby let her eyes fall shut as he continued to talk about The Roast.

When she awoke, she found that a blanket was covering her as she sat in the chair on the porch. Glancing down, she saw a note beside her empty cup of coffee.

You look amazing when you sleep. See you soon. The note was signed with an XO. Abby smiled, and a warmth washed over her. It was an almost painfully hopeful feeling that she hadn't felt in a long time.

CHAPTER
17

Raelynn was just walking out of the office when Chief Austin pulled up. Part of her wanted to comment on his tardiness, but she figured it was none of her business that he was late—again. Trying to be patient, she waited for him to get out of his car so she could fill him in on what she knew about the case so far. The chief looked weary as if he had the weight of the world on his shoulders. She had to admit that this murder affected their whole department. She was sure the chief felt the same.

As the pair stood in front of the station, Raelynn explained her thoughts on the case but could see the skepticism in the lines of Chief Austin's face. Clearly, he wasn't fully committed. Raelynn reluctantly understood. She wasn't buying it 100 percent either, but then again, it was just a theory.

"I guess I need to check up on Mr. Ball's alibi as a next step," Raelynn sighed, kicking sullenly at the ground. He said he was with his girlfriend, Abby Jones, but she's not from around here."

"Abby Jones?" Chief Austin glanced up in surprise. "There was an Abby Jones at the coffee shop earlier. She said she just got into town and is staying at a house near the quarry."

Raelynn arched an eyebrow at the chief. "How the heck do you know that?"

"I'm the chief. It's part of my role to introduce myself to newcomers to Seneca Rocks. Gotta make sure they're not getting into any trouble around here." Chief Austin winked before waltzing into the station, leaving Raelynn standing alone out front.

With a tiny sigh of frustration, Raelynn returned to her vehicle without even entering the station. Back in her cruiser, she headed north across town. It had been years since she had been by the quarry, but she knew there weren't a lot of houses out that way. This place should be reasonably easy to find.

During the drive, instead of dwelling endlessly on the case, Raelynn took the time to enjoy the scenery. As she sped down the freeway, she passed miles and miles of fields getting ready to be planted with corn, the major crop grown in these parts. If a field didn't have a crop, then it was used to pasture livestock, typically cattle and sheep. To her delight, Raelynn also drove by a pasture full of cattle with new calves that had been recently born. She loved this time of year because of all the baby animals. Her heart melted at the sight of the calves and lambs prancing and playing around together. Life was so precious.

As Raelynn passed the entrance to the limestone quarry, she groaned in dismay. So much for having a clean cruiser. The road dust created a thin layer over her vehicle as she kicked up dirt and small rocks with her tires.

Although she'd had no interest in the quarry since college, it was still in operation. Her father had worked there for as long as she could remember. He'd been an explosives handler and had wired the quarry to blow in preparation for digging limestone. He had been getting ready to retire and was even training an apprentice when the accident happened. Since then, Raelynn couldn't face going into the quarry, and so far, she'd never had a reason to.

Just past the entrance sat a little white house. Raelynn slowed and took it in. She knew that Abby had to live around here somewhere. So she decided to pull into the gravel driveway and at least ask the resident if they knew her.

A moment later, Raelynn pulled the cruiser to a stop behind a gray Volkswagen Beetle. After exiting the cruiser, she casually made her way around the car. As she was approaching the house, she glanced back one last time. At this point, she was positive she had the right house. On the front of the Beetle was a customized license plate with "ABBY" written in red font. Well, she should be home since her car was here.

Raelynn took her time assessing her surroundings. The outside of the house was clean, and the porch was decorated for spring with two rocking chairs with matching pillows and blankets. Cute. Maybe Raelynn could get her to come to her house and decorate. She just didn't have the energy to do it herself. A red front door greeted guests. Raelynn didn't see a doorbell, so she knocked and waited. And waited. And waited. She had just turned around to leave when she heard the door slowly creak open.

"May I help you?"

Raelynn saw a petite girl with long, dark hair through the small crack of the open door. She had a hard time guessing her age, but she suspected she was in her twenties. "Hello. Are you Abby Jones?"

A look of surprise appeared on the young lady's face. Obviously, she wasn't expecting anyone to know her. "Yes," was her only response. The girl looked scared to death. She wasn't an attractive girl, but she had a friendly face.

"I have some questions to ask you about Thomas," Raelynn said, taking a step forward. She was hoping to be invited into the house. Otherwise, they could sit on the porch together. Regardless, they needed to have a conversation.

"I'm afraid I don't understand," Abby replied in a reserved tone. "How could I know anything about Thomas?"

Raelynn needed to get Abby to trust her, or she wouldn't get any useful information from her. "Why don't you come out and have a seat on the porch and we can talk?"

She took the lead, traipsing over to the rocking chairs and taking a seat. Then, she waited patiently as Abby made her decision and joined her in the opposite chair. With trembling hands, Abby reached for the blanket and placed it across her lap. Raelynn watched as she nervously twisted the material between her fingers, rocking back and forth in her seat.

"I'll start by introducing myself. I'm Detective Bailey with the Seneca Rocks Police Department. I was told that you know Thomas Ball. Is that correct?" Raelynn asked.

"Yes, I guess you could say I know him." Abby's voice was tired and faint. *She's definitely shy*, Raelynn thought.

"How long have you known Thomas?" Raelynn believed it was appropriate at this point to refer to him as Abby did.

"Well, I've been talking to him for about two years," Abby replied.

Wow, Raelynn couldn't believe how vague Abby was at answering her questions. "Okay," she said with a nod of encouragement. Then, she decided to try a different angle. "Why don't you tell me a little bit about yourself?"

Instantly, Abby became defensive. "Why do you need to know about me? I haven't done anything." That was an interesting comment, especially when Raelynn hadn't even told Abby why she wanted information about Thomas.

"Look, I'm not here about you, but at least give some basic information so I know I am talking to the right person," Raelynn snapped. She could feel her temper start to climb. That was one thing that could get in her way. She had learned to control her anger with people, but some just rubbed her the wrong way. She was an officer of the law. Shouldn't people respect her authority when she came around asking questions? It's not like it wasn't for a good reason.

Abby stared at her while she contemplated the request. "Alright," she finally said. "My name is Abby Jones—well, Abbigail Jones. I've known Thomas about two years now."

Raelynn let out a breath that she'd been unaware she was holding in. "Thanks, Abby. Let's start from the beginning. Tell me how you met Thomas."

By all appearances, Abby did not want to talk about Thomas, but she grudgingly relented. "We met online through a cooking chat room. We would swap recipes. Eventually, we started sending emails to each other."

"Wait a sec. You said you met him online . . . so where exactly are you from?" Raelynn inquired.

Abby slowly raised her eyes to Raelynn's and shook her head. "I'm from Kentucky," was all that Abby allowed herself to say. Once again, more vague information.

"So how did you end up here in West Virginia?" Raelynn pressed.

"I came to see Thomas."

Abby refused to be more forthcoming, and Raelynn could feel her ire start to rise. She repositioned herself in the rocking chair, giving herself and Abby a minute to think. "Okay, so you met him online while you were in Kentucky. Is that right?"

Abby nodded her head in response.

"When did you come to Seneca Rocks?" Raelynn started again with her line of questioning.

"I've been here a couple days," Abby replied without making eye contact. She kept fidgeting with her blanket.

Raelynn took a minute to register what Abby had just said. If her memory served her correctly, Mr. Ball had used Abby as his alibi for when Kate was murdered. Except that had been over the weekend, and Abby wasn't in Seneca Rocks yet according to her story.

As Raelynn sat there processing the information, she took in Abby's presence. She was definitely hiding something. Raelynn's impression was that she was a meek individual who didn't want to draw attention to herself. That would partially explain the ambiguous answers. But what was she trying to keep under wraps?

"Let me get this straight. You've only been in town a couple of days. Have you seen Thomas since you got here?" Maybe Thomas had his timeline screwed up. Raelynn needed more information to determine what was going on here.

"No. Actually, I've been sending him emails, but I haven't gotten a reply. I've been thinking I came all this way, and he wasn't even real." Abby finally gazed up at Raelynn with glassy eyes. Was she starting to cry? Obviously, she believed that Thomas was real, and she wanted to meet him.

"So it's safe to say that you weren't with him over the weekend." Raelynn wasn't really asking—more like confirming it with her.

"No. I told you I've only been here a couple days. I don't understand why you are asking me these questions. Why do you think I was with Thomas?" Abby started to fidget even more in her chair, which was slightly tipped forward. She cuddled the blanket closer, looking like a child holding her favorite teddy bear for security.

Raelynn figured she might as well fill her in on what was going on. "Abby, Thomas said he was with his girlfriend over the weekend. He specifically stated it was you."

"Why would Thomas say that? I haven't even met him in real life yet." Abby was definitely flustered by what Raelynn had just said.

"Well, Abby, a past girlfriend of Thomas's was found murdered over the weekend. He used you as his alibi." Raelynn waited a beat, letting what she had just said sink in.

Suddenly, Abby seemed to comprehend the reason Raelynn was asking her these questions. Sitting up straighter in the rocking chair, she looked Raelynn right in the face with wide eyes. "You're saying that Thomas may have killed that girl?" Now it was time for Abby to ask the questions. "You can't be serious?"

"Well, that's why I'm here. To confirm his alibi—which actually can't be done," Raelynn replied. "Do you think Thomas may have killed her?" Raelynn pressed.

"What do you mean? How would I know?" Abby responded, startled.

"You said you knew him for two years. Does he seem like the type of person that would kill an ex-girlfriend?"

"How would I know? I only chatted with him online," Abby responded flatly, a sense of stubbornness clearly setting in.

"But you came here to meet with him, right? So, obviously, you had some feelings for him. Was he acting different from normal?" An exasperated tone had begun coloring her voice. Raelynn thought that Abby knew more about Thomas than she was letting on. Why would someone talk to a person for two years and move to the same area as him without really knowing anything about him? Raelynn wasn't buying this for a minute.

"Yeah, I guess so. I mean, I started developing feelings for him the more I talked to him. He paid attention to me. I felt that he really got me. So we sort of planned for me to visit him, but we didn't have a set date for me to come to West Virginia."

"So you said you haven't talked to him for a while, right?" Raelynn asked again.

"Yeah. I've been emailing him since I arrived, but I haven't gotten a response."

"What are you going to do if Thomas never answers you?" Raelynn inquired.

"Gee." Abby glanced out across the front lawn. "I haven't really thought about it like that. I like it here, and I saw that the coffee shop is hiring. Maybe I'll do that."

"That position at the coffee shop was Kate's. She's the girl that was murdered," Raelynn explained.

"Oh." Abby's face grew solemn. "I'm sure I can find something in this town."

The two sat in their rocking chairs, looking out across the lawn. Feeling as if she'd gotten some answers but a whole lot more questions, Raelynn took one last look at Abby and rose from her seat.

"Well, I'll let you get back to what you were doing," she stated, moving across the small porch toward her cruiser. "Thanks for taking the time to talk to me."

Abby continued to fidget with the blanket on her lap and stare past Raelynn. This conversation had probably put a big hiccup in the plans she'd had with Thomas Ball. Now that Raelynn had confirmed he wasn't with Abby on the day Kate was murdered, he'd essentially cemented his place at the top of her suspect list. Her next step was to bring him in for official questioning.

"By the way, how did you end up at this place?" Raelynn asked abruptly.

Abby mentally considered what the man had told her before responding in a would-be-casual tone. "Oh, I found it online. Must be a vacation rental."

Raelynn shook her head. "Well, thanks again." With a slight jerk of her head, she walked off, leaving Abby looking small and forlorn by herself on the porch.

CHAPTER
18

Sleep never came easily for Raelynn. She was used to never getting the required amount of rest, not only due to the crazy hours working for the police department but because she always seemed to be fighting demons after her dad's death. Often, she would find that she'd fallen asleep in her dad's favorite chair after drinking too much or, like a few nights previously, she would pass out while taking her bath.

Truth be told, Raelynn hated herself for drinking. She knew she had a problem but didn't want to admit it. Raelynn cringed every time she arrested someone for intoxication, admonishing them that they needed to learn to control their drinking. Boy! How many times has she told that to people she'd arrested? She knew she should really hold herself to a higher standard.

At the very least, she should make a change in order to improve her social life. She couldn't remember the last time she'd gone on a date, let alone the last time she had been in a serious relationship. Of course, now that she was working a case that seemed to have a love—or at least sexual—connection, it put a whole different perspective on romance for her. How could something that was supposed to be fun, caring, and meaningful result in such a horrible consequence?

Mind wandering, Raelynn looked around at her family home. She hadn't touched anything since her father's death. The same family photos were still hanging on the walls. She even had the same quilt on her bed. Maybe it was time for a change. She needed to move on, and now seemed as good a time as any.

As she sat looking over the crime scene photos spread out on her coffee table, Raelynn reached over and opened her second beer. Change was a part of life . . . she could do it. It was time she made some changes. First would be to make the house hers. Then, she decided she would get a new wardrobe. If she felt that was good, maybe she would even consider changing up her hair. She'd always been told that a new color and cut could completely change one's mood. She had just always been too scared to go outside her comfort zone.

Perhaps unsurprisingly, all her life, Raelynn had been deemed a tomboy. Without siblings, she had been the apple of her parents' eyes—but not spoiled. Since her parents valued independence and self-sufficiency, she had been raised to take care of herself. She was pretty handy, was confident handling a gun, and knew how to keep a house. Her mom had also taught her how to cook when she was young, a skill that went to good use when her mother got sick and eventually passed away from cancer. Raelynn was a freshman and had to grow up fast. She had helped take care of her mother after her diagnosis, just like her mother used to take care of her. Then, when her mom succumbed to her illness, Raelynn took care of her dad as he grieved the loss of his life partner.

Despite his grief, her dad made a point to connect with Raelynn as they navigated life together without her mom. She remembered when he had bought her a car for the first time. It had been a stick shift, and she had been so excited. Her dad had made her detail it, check the oil, and learn how to change a tire before he handed over the keys. Raelynn knew she had to take care of it to make her dad proud.

Ultimately, she learned valuable skills and life lessons from both of her parents. Raelynn looked a lot like her mother with the same complexion and build; however, her attitude was inherited from her father. Raelynn was often frank and to the point. She wasn't afraid to say what was on her mind. Of course, being a police officer had taught Raelynn how to control her tongue. There was a time and place for everything, and Raelynn had finally figured that out. Still, her default was to be blunt and upfront—just like her dad had been.

Shaking away her suddenly melancholy thoughts, Raelynn glanced down at the photos and brought herself back to reality. She still had that nagging feeling that she was missing something. She was sure of it. To organize her thoughts, she had a notebook handy to keep track of the evidence as results came in, and she perused it with intense concentration. The dump site for the body had been a location where it was guaranteed that someone would find it eventually. Although, if it hadn't been hunting season, it would have taken longer to find Kate.

Absently rubbing her temple, Raelynn picked up Kate's crime scene photos with her other hand. She remembered the broken branch. Although the other officers hadn't seemed interested in it, Raelynn had written it down on her notepad to follow up on that. Despite the lack of evidence confirming its relevance, she wasn't entirely content with ruling out the old barn not too far away as well. Checking her notes, she verified that she still had no information from the county clerk (as if she had forgotten). It could not possibly take this long to run a property check. Determined to get answers, she made it a top priority to visit the county clerk again tomorrow morning. In fact, she would make it a personal visit.

Raelynn also hadn't heard anything more from Darla about Kate's results. She would swing by her house tomorrow and see if she could catch her before she went into work at the hospital. It had been a while since she had been there anyway. It would be nice to have a girls day, but she knew they would end up talking about the case.

She was so glad she had a friend such as Darla, and she was happy that she'd facilitated the match with her and Monte. There was quite an age difference between the two, but it didn't seem to bother them or anyone else for that matter. Both of their working lifestyles fit into their marriage. Some people couldn't stand to be away from each other, but those two had been single for so long that they had gotten into a routine. It was sometimes rare for them to see each other outside of their busy schedules, but they made it work.

The time they did get to spend with each other they cherished deeply. In fact, they would arrange their schedules to take vacations a couple of times a year so they could have solid quality time. Raelynn had even joined them once but had felt like a third wheel the entire time. She realized they needed to spend time together without a tagalong.

When Raelynn next looked at the clock, she was shocked at the time, not having realized how late it had gotten. She grabbed her almost empty beer bottle and decided to call it a night. She knew there was one part of her routine that she would never change—her bath before bed. Raelynn loved the old clawfoot tub in the bathroom. It would never leave. She often took a book with her and allowed herself to get caught up in the story, happily forgetting about the happenings of her life. She would read for so long that the water would turn tepid, and she would rush through the rest of her bath before she got goosebumps.

Eager to indulge in her favorite nighttime activity, she drew a hot bath and let herself sink into the thick layer of bubbles. As her skin turned pink from the heat of the water, Raelynn let her mind relax, and soon, she found tears running down her face. Being forced to go to the quarry was what she'd needed. Somehow, it had provided some sense of closure. She had been denying herself this for far too long. At least that's what she was telling herself. She would never forget her dad and how much he meant to her, but by facing the place that reminded her of her father most, she'd finally let herself be at peace.

"Tomorrow's a new day," Raelynn murmured to herself. That much was true, but she had no idea just what tomorrow was going to bring.

CHAPTER
19

Since Kate's death, Thomas had been in a state of shock. He had turned off his phone and basically become a recluse. The truth was he had been in love with Kate. He'd known it back when she was still in high school.

The relationship got serious fast. They were able to keep it hidden, but they had a feeling that rumors were starting to surface. Thomas knew that if anyone found out, he would end up in prison for a very long time, but it was a chance he was willing to take.

It wasn't until after Adam's death that Kate began acting strange. She would miss class, and on an increasingly frequent basis, he would find her at his apartment when he got home from school. Even more alarming, she would sometimes talk like she was out of her mind, indicating she was seeing ghosts, and she rarely slept.

Thomas was concerned for her but unsure of what exactly to do. He figured a deep depression had just set in and he needed to let it run its course. But Kate just kept slipping. The whole school felt sorry for her. Something as tragic and senseless as Adam's death hadn't happened in the community before, so they just swept her behavior under the rug. Everyone just hoped she would pull through it.

Thomas had told the lady detective that he'd broken it off because she'd become too serious. That was a lie. He actually hadn't liked what Kate had become. She neglected to take care of herself. He had to beg her to take a shower. She wore the same clothes all week. The dark circles under her eyes told him she hadn't slept. He hid her away inside his apartment and tried to make her presentable before she left. It was like taking care of child he didn't have.

He'd ended it one evening when Kate had seemed unaware that he was even there. He had never seen her so spaced out before. At the time, Thomas didn't know what was happening, but he wanted no part of it anymore. So he'd told her it was over and that she had to leave. She didn't get mad, which was what he had expected. Instead, she simply seemed disappointed. Like someone else had given up on her. Thomas hadn't seen her after that. As he'd told the detective, he'd made sure to stay clear of the café when he found out she was working there. He didn't want to do anything that would make it seem like he was still interested in her. Although that sounded cruel and maybe a little self-centered, he wanted to make sure the ties were cut. Plus, it might have been even more cruel to keep showing up in her face if he wasn't willing to reinitiate the relationship.

That was why Thomas had started exploring online dating in the first place. He'd thought that if he kept his mind interested in something or someone else, he wouldn't fall back to Kate. But he hadn't wanted to rely on the traditional way of finding a date. In fact, he'd gotten lucky through a cooking blog where everyone would swap recipes and discuss questions and tips.

That's where he'd met Abby. He didn't know a lot about her at first, but it was apparent that she loved to cook and craved the conversation from everyone on the blog. She'd seemed shy in the way that she really didn't talk about herself much but was intrigued about everyone else. For his part, Thomas was intrigued by her and asked if they could exchange emails. To his delight, she seemed more than eager to comply.

He wasn't sure how long they'd been exchanging emails, but it had been a long time. Abby seemed comfortable with him and eventually started sharing personal details. For example, he'd discovered that she lived in Kentucky. Plus, she'd divulged that she was married to her high school sweetheart. When she'd told him that, he'd pulled back slightly, a little wary about continuing the chatting, even though he had no intention of ever meeting her. At that point, she was more like a friend to talk to. But he enjoyed the connection with Abby too much to give it up, so the conversations continued.

In fact, Thomas had reciprocated by telling Abby he was a teacher who lived in West Virginia. Over time, he grew to depend on her more and more, and as he continued to confide in her, their relationship deepened. What had begun as an online friendship had unmistakably turned into something more intimate. At least, as intimate as you can get with someone else online.

Now, with everything going on, Thomas felt bad because when he'd learned that Kate had died, he'd put everything else to the side, including Abby. He didn't even feel like reaching out to her for support, even though he knew in the back of his mind that he should ask Abby to validate his alibi. Unfortunately, he just couldn't face anyone right now. He had to get his head on straight first. In a small town such as Seneca Rocks, rumors spread quickly. He couldn't risk people noticing he was taking Kate's death harder than a teacher who hadn't even had her in class should. Even worse, there was no doubt the police already had him on their suspect list. Even though the detective hadn't explicitly stated that, he knew that's what was going on. Although he knew that he hadn't killed Kate, he realized he somehow needed to prove it to them.

Thomas turned on his cell phone and noted he didn't have a whole lot of missed calls. He was too much of a loner. However, he did see the school had called—probably to see where he was since he simply hadn't shown up that day. Shaking his head, he decided to deal with that later. For now, he was going to check his email. To his alarm, he realized he had numerous messages from Abby. Shame suffused him, and he instantly regretted his decision to cut off communication. Randomly picking a message from the day before, he started reading.

Thomas sat in shock at the discovery that Abby had taken steps to break free of her old life. His jaw hanging open, he sat on his couch, opening each email and reading the progress. Thomas felt like such an idiot, not to mention a jerk, for not responding. He was the one person Abby could count on, and he had been so wrapped up in his own pain that he had let her down.

From what he could tell, Abby had carefully planned an escape from her abusive husband and was headed to meet Thomas. Maybe he wasn't too late? Seneca Rocks was such a small town. Maybe he could find her. Surely someone would have noticed her by now. In a community like this, strangers couldn't stay in the vicinity without gaining the attention of the locals. Struck with a new sense of determination, Thomas resolved to devote the following day to finding his online girlfriend. He couldn't save Kate, but maybe he could save Abby.

With quick movements, Thomas gathered his keys and wallet and approached the front door. He yanked it open and took a step back.

"Hello, Thomas. I'm glad I caught you."

Thomas hadn't been expecting to see her, but somehow, he wasn't surprised either.

CHAPTER
20

The chief sat at his kitchen table, reading the local newspaper, while the love of his life, Carrie, made him breakfast. His normal routine was to read the sports section first. Then, if he had time, he would go on to the local news. Today, he chose to steer clear of the news. He knew it would still be covering Kate's death, and right now, they hadn't uncovered much. Gazing over the edge of the paper, he watched while his wife put his bacon and eggs on his plate. How could anyone kill someone they had been intimate with? He loved his wife, and no matter how difficult their marriage and family situation became, he could never lay a hand on her. He supposed that was the difference between normal and psycho.

He knew Carrie had been worried about him and the other officers investigating this heinous crime. This type of thing just didn't happen in a small town like Seneca Rocks . . . until now. He would be lying to himself if he said it wasn't having an effect on them. Of course, this line of work affected everyone differently. He'd been keeping an eye on his officers, especially Raelynn. He knew she'd been going through a lot with her father's death and was concerned this investigation would just keep her from addressing the grief issues she needed to overcome. Plus, despite her efforts to hide it or treat it as a nonchalant thing, he was aware of her drinking. When they got this case solved, he was going to make her take some time off. Maybe suggest a therapist. Whatever he could do to get her on a healthier track.

Carrie took the seat next to him, setting his breakfast on his place mat, and gently took the newspaper away from him. "Are you okay?" she asked softly.

He turned his face away from her and answered as honestly as he could. "I'm not sure," was all that he could say.

Carrie gave him a little smile like she always did. It was reassuring and understanding. Reaching over, he brought her hand to his mouth and placed a light kiss across her knuckles. This simple gesture was something that had lasted throughout their relationship.

The chief had met Carrie after he'd left the military. He hadn't grown up in this area, but he'd been stationed at an active naval base in the next county over for four years and had fallen in love with the area. He'd also fallen in love with Carrie. At the time, she'd worked at the local pharmacy as a tech. He'd gotten a horrible cold one winter and went in to grab some over-the-counter meds, hoping to deal with the symptoms himself instead of going through the rigamarole of visiting a doctor. He had been contemplating two different meds when she'd walked up to him and grabbed one out of his hand.

"This one won't do you any good. You need a decongestant, not a cough suppressant," she'd instructed, looking him straight in the eyes. She was smiling that reassuring smile, and he was hooked. Once he could breathe on his own again, he had asked her out, and they hadn't been apart since.

From there, he had joined the police department and risen rapidly through the ranks. By now, he had been the chief for quite a few years, but he'd been secretly thinking about retirement. He and Carrie deserved a break. Soon enough, the twins would be graduating college and pursuing their own ambitions. Maybe it was time to hand the reigns over to someone else. But that was the hard part—trying to decide who that should be. He had a few capable officers that could manage the department, but he'd narrowed it down to two: Raelynn and Monte. They both had good qualities but operated day to day on a completely different scale.

Monte was so laidback. He took each situation he encountered at a slow and methodical pace. A deep thinker, he was quiet and introspective, happy to sit on a situation for weeks, analyzing it from all possible angles before giving his opinion. That could be a great quality in investigations—not rushing to conclusions. Monte did not act on impulse. He was very calculated. However, the chief knew better than anyone that, sometimes, you need to be able to make quick decisions and provide commands. As a chief, the public and your officers are relying on you to guide them. Monte needed to work on that skill.

On the other hand, Raelynn had great investigative abilities. With no hesitation, she consistently dove deep into the evidence until she found that one clue that was overlooked. Of course, she did need to learn to relax and step back from the situation sometimes. She often got caught up in cases and struggled to detach. However, she was great at giving commands and getting things accomplished. She probably had the highest closure rate in the whole department—that's why she'd been promoted to detective. Seneca Rocks really didn't have enough priority crimes to warrant the position, but the chief saw potential in her and wanted to see where that potential could lead.

All in all, it really didn't matter at this point; he wasn't retiring anytime soon. Plus, he wanted to see who would prove themselves in this investigation. Both Raelynn and Monte would be put in the spotlight, and he was interested in seeing who would shine brightest. Finishing his hearty meal, the chief stood up from the kitchen table and kissed his wife on the forehead. Then, he grabbed his gun belt and walked out the door, wondering what the new day would bring.

CHAPTER
21

Abby opened her eyes to a bright morning, fingers of sunlight combing across her pillow through the open blinds. She'd been sleeping so soundly that, now that she was awake, she didn't want to get up. So, with a tired sigh, she pulled the covers closer to her to create a cozy cocoon.

West Virginia was a lot like Kentucky this time of year—chilly in the mornings. The blankets could only do so much to keep her warm. So, after a few minutes, she resigned herself to getting up. Flinging her legs over the edge of the bed, she bent down to pull on a pair of sweatpants. Glancing at the clock on the way to the bathroom, she noted the time. Eight thirty a.m. If she were still with Nate, she would have been up for three hours by now. She would have made him his breakfast and lunch and sent him to work. Why must she still think about him?

In front of the bathroom mirror, Abby took a long look at herself. She didn't love what she saw, but she didn't hate it either. Her new life was giving her a new sense of confidence, and that was beginning to radiate from her. Maybe she was holding herself differently. Or maybe she was just seeing herself differently for the first time. After shrugging and then making a face at herself in the mirror, she turned on the cold water and splashed some on her face. It was a new day, and she was going to make the best of it. After brushing her teeth, she added just a hint of makeup to her face and tied her hair into a neatly stacked bun on top of her head. Overall, she was pleased with the effect. Maybe she was prettier than she gave herself credit for. She hoped she looked good today at least because she wanted to head over to the café and talk to Mickey about a job. Today was the day that would change her life.

As Abby was trying to find an appropriate outfit in the limited clothing options she had available to her, she heard gravel crunching in the driveway again. Stepping up to the window, she peeked through the curtains and felt her face light up as she saw him step out of the car and approach her front porch. Once again, he was carrying two cups of coffee. Still wearing her sweatpants, she raced to the door, and before he could knock, she opened it with a welcoming grin.

"I didn't know if you would be awake or not, but I thought I would take the chance," he said as he handed her one of the coffees. Accepting it graciously, Abby motioned for him to take a seat on the porch. It was quickly becoming her favorite place, especially when she got to talk to him while sitting side by side in twin rocking chairs. Abby took a seat in the rocker beside him and draped the blanket across her shoulders. Then, she took the coffee cup in both hands, luxuriating in the warmth it provided. Taking a deep breath, she inhaled the fantastic fragrance of java.

"Are you just getting off work?" she asked after taking a quick gulp.

"Yeah, I thought I would check on you on my way home," he replied.

"That's awful kind of you. I've never had someone take so much interest in me," Abby stated. She meant for it to sound flippant or perhaps even flirty, but instead, it came across as almost... longing.

"Why not?" he inquired. Cheeks reddening in faint embarrassment, she shook her head and stared out over the lawn. "You know you can talk to me, right?" he reassured her.

Abby took another small sip of her coffee and answered in a shy manner. "The man I was with before—he was controlling. I'm sure he loved me—at least at the beginning of our relationship he did. I think it got to the point where he was obsessive about me. He fell out of love with me, but he wanted to control everything I did. He wasn't like that when we were dating or even right after we got married; however, he just changed overnight it seemed. He stopped me from hanging out with my friends. He bought my clothes for me. He would only let me out of the house when I could go with him. He literally controlled *everything* I did," she explained.

"And that's why you left?" he asked gently.

"I had to. I had gotten into such a deep depression that I had to find a way out," she replied. "No one knew what was going on. It was me and Nate's secret, you know, how he treated me. It took a while for me to get away, and when I got the chance, I ran. I couldn't live like that anymore."

Abby raised her eyes and looked at his face. He was so handsome, and he patiently sat there listening to her. No one had ever been so attentive to her. To Nate, her opinion didn't matter, and she'd long ago learned to keep her mouth shut around him. She thought back to getting involved in the food blog. She'd been able to express herself there, even if only in writing. She could make even the most boring dishes seem sophisticated to the point she could almost smell it cooking when she read the recipe.

Attempting to shake away the memories, Abby took another sip of her coffee and let the strong smell waft through her senses. As she closed her eyes, she felt his hand slip inside hers.

"Don't worry. Your story can be our secret," she heard him say as she slipped into darkness.

CHAPTER
22

Abby didn't know how long she had been asleep, but when she woke, she found herself back in her bedroom. She was groggy, her head hurt, and she could barely open her eyes. To her surprise, when Abby tried to raise her head and sit up, she realized she couldn't. It was like she had a huge weight on her body holding her down. The pressure was so much it almost took her breath away.

Abby slowly turned her head to the right. Even the slightest move made the room spin. Once she could focus, she realized the curtains on the lone window were shut tight. No light could be seen. What time was it? How did she end up here in bed? Perplexed and still fuzzy headed, she couldn't figure out what was happening. After a moment, Abby's eyes roamed to the top of the bed. She could see an arm was tied to the headboard. She lay staring at the bound wrist, struggling to comprehend that it was her own. Why couldn't she feel her upper extremities? She willed her hand and fingers to move, but nothing happened.

Slowly realizing something was amiss, Abby turned her head to the other side, noting that her other hand was bound the same way to the headboard. *What is happening?* Squinting at the red paint on her fingernails, she knew without a doubt that it was she who was tied up. *But why?* She tried again to move her hands, yet no matter how hard she concentrated, nothing happened. She was simply numb.

As Abby struggled to come to terms with reality, she heard a faint rustling. Frightened but wanting to find some answers, she let her eyes glide toward the direction of the noise. He was there, sitting on the edge of her bed. Once again, she tried to get up but failed. The bindings around her hands were cutting into her flesh, containing any movement she tried to make.

"What's happening?" Abby released with a silent cry.

He slowly turned his head her way when she spoke, a blank stare on his face. It was like he was looking through her instead of at her. Frightened and bewildered, Abby's eyes followed the slow progression of his hand as he reached out and touched her leg. Her mind registered what he was doing, but she couldn't feel his touch. Still numb. He slowly slid his hand up her thigh, eventually coming to a stop on her belly. Abby's eyes took in the red that lay beneath his hand. What was she wearing? Glancing in horror at the rest of her body, she realized she was no longer wearing the clothes she'd had on when sitting on the porch. Instead, she was wearing a scrap of red lingerie. Mind spinning with possible explanations, she frantically considered how this could have happened, but in the end, she decided there was only one possible conclusion. He must have changed her clothes while she was asleep.

"You're so beautiful," he said, bringing Abby out of her state of shock. She looked at him with wide eyes, dumbfounded by his behavior. He was staring intently at her body.

"Why are you doing this?" Abby whispered. She strained against the restraints around her wrists, mentally willing them to release their death grip on her. Still, the only movement that she could manage was turning her head. Abby's eyes wandered around the room, looking for anything that could help her. The windows had been covered, and the bedroom door was shut. Unless she could escape her restraints, she knew she would have to endure whatever he had planned.

Fortunately, Abby was good at living through challenging and even unbearable situations. She hadn't survived living with Nate that long without being smart. So, as the fog lifted from her brain, she swiftly considered a variety of strategies, thinking maybe she could distract him.

"I'm glad you came over today. I really wanted to see you," she began hesitantly, watching closely to see if there were any changes in his behavior. There was essentially no reaction. His hand just kept caressing her stomach as if he were trying to memorize her through his fingertips. In fact, she saw no indication that he'd even heard her, so she tried again.

"How did you know that red was my favorite color?" This statement made him pause. Abby watched his eyes slide up to her face as a smile slowly crept onto his face. She finally had his attention; now she just had to keep it the only way she knew how.

"I really like what you bought for me. I would have definitely picked this out for us to enjoy too," she continued in a soothing tone. She needed to keep him focused on what she was saying. She figured her best chance of getting out of this was to let him know that she was okay with what he wanted from her and that he didn't need to do it this way.

"It doesn't take a genius to figure out what you like," he replied. Taken aback by this comment, Abby hesitated, her mind churning with the effort of coming up with an appropriate response. He was gazing intently at her, his eyes almost black. Abby let out a strained chuckle. She had meant for the laugh to be a cute giggle, but under the circumstances, she hadn't quite been able to pull it off.

"You know, I was hoping our relationship would progress to this stage. I felt it," Abby tried again. This time he chuckled, deep and throaty, and she was abruptly uncertain whether this was the right direction to go.

Originally, she'd hoped that if she invited his intended actions, he would lose the desire to actually carry them out. He would feel that he was no longer in control and that his plan had failed. At this point, she knew the inevitable would come. She just wanted to put it off as long as possible. Maybe she would start getting feeling in her body again, and maybe she would be able to work her way out of the restraints. Abby was smart. She knew in her heart she could get out of this. She was so close to her wonderful new life—fresh, fulfilling, *free*. She couldn't get derailed now—not by this cruel twist of fate. Why had she trusted this man—this stranger—when he'd offered to help her?

Abby watched as he returned his attention to her body. His hands trailed over her, slowly moving to her breasts, exposing them from their lace confinement. She helplessly bore witness to his actions, still not feeling his fingers caress her nipples. Abby knew she had little command or attention over him. She could see her chest rising with each breath she took. She was nearly hyperventilating at that point as silent panic started to overcome her.

It seemed like time stood still. She didn't know how long he followed her body with his touch. His hands wandered back down her form. Then, he stood, unzipped his pants, and lowered them to ground, all while keeping his eyes locked on her. Petrified, Abby let out a low whimper, fully aware of what was about to happen. Creeping on top of her, he pressed his mouth to hers, delicately at first. Before long, however, he was kissing her intensely, and Abby had no way of fighting him. He gently kissed her forehead before leaving a trail of kisses down her body. Stomach roiling, Abby closed her eyes on the horrific scene and began saying a silent prayer, glad that she couldn't feel what was happening to her.

She didn't know how long she lay there waiting for it to be over. It wasn't until she felt a crushing weight on her throat that she opened her eyes. His hands were wrapped around her neck, squeezing her windpipe. She could feel the pressure from within but couldn't feel his fingers on her. Desperate to escape, she tried to shake her head out of his grasp, but he was much too strong. Gradually, her fight for air seemed to fade. Different colored spots began filling Abby's vision as she struggled to take a breath. Her vision became blurry, and his face kept going in and out of focus.

Abby knew this was it. She had lost so much. First, her identity. Then, her husband. And now, her life.

CHAPTER
23

On the ride into town, the chief continued contemplating his retirement. At breakfast, he had thought it would be a long way off, but now, he couldn't stop thinking about it. He had been in this game too long. He really wasn't ready to handle the shake-up created by this investigation either. He liked the quiet little town that he called home, but he was afraid there was more going on than he suspected.

He knew he had a good department full of officers. Most of them were young and doing their best to make a name for themselves. Choosing to be a police officer was not easy. Every day, they had to make the decision to help others while at the same time putting their life on the line. Obviously, in a small town like Seneca Rocks, officers were not in fear for their life all the time; however, they did encounter some instances that turned for the worse quickly.

The best quality of an officer was their voice. It was not the sound of the voice that mattered, it was the tone. Officers learned to communicate with others by using different types of tones. In an emotional situation, one would use a quieter tone to show empathy. There were instances, though, when a situation could get out of control, and it was the responsibility of the officer to regain control of the situation. Therefore, the officer's tone would have to be deep and demanding. The chief knew his officers were able to relate to whatever situation they were in, and the results rarely turned violent.

The chief was still trying to learn more about his officers too. Some, like Tony, were real quiet and didn't do much outside of work. Dane was more of a clown, but he was still deeply devoted to his job. In fact, the younger guys breathed and slept police work. He was afraid they'd eventually find Seneca Rocks too calm and look elsewhere for more action. On the other hand, Raelynn and Monte would never leave. He was sure of it. They'd both grown up here and both would die here.

Monte Anderson and his family were Native American Cherokee. That tribe had long ago settled in Seneca Rocks; however, most had ultimately traveled elsewhere.

Monte's parents operated the state wildlife and historical museum. It housed a plethora of creatures found around Seneca Rocks, all mostly killed by local townspeople. Monte's mother took pride in displaying her own housewares, rugs, and baskets that her ancestors made over time. Since Monte and Darla didn't have any children, the traditions were told to outsiders in hopes they would preserve and honor the Cherokee culture.

During fall festivals in Seneca Rocks and surrounding towns, the Andersons would show up in traditional Cherokee dress and perform ritual ceremonies. Often, they would set up a nice campfire and demonstrate how to make fry bread. Mickey had been hounding them for months to supply the café with some, but they assured him that was too commercial for their taste.

Monte had joined the police force right after the chief. He wasn't a bad officer by any means, but sometimes, he seemed to lack motivation. He had been a sergeant on night shift for close to twenty years and had shown no clear desire to change.

The chief hadn't broached the subject much because he ran his department with designated shifts. He believed messing with people's sleeping habits and home lives would result in disgruntled employees. So officers would bid on shifts when they were hired and would only change if necessary.

Monte's night shift seemed to work for him and Darla. As a nurse at the local hospital, she typically worked nights or evenings, although she had twelve-hour shifts compared to his eight-hour ones. All in all, their lifestyle and routines seemed to work well for them. They could often be seen at the diner together in the evenings, grabbing some dinner before starting their shifts. It was sweet that they valued their independence but cherished their quality time together too.

If the chief remembered correctly, Darla had been born in Seneca Rocks, but right after high school, she'd left to get her registered nursing degree. She'd eventually made it back and bought a place just far enough out of town and away from her parents to have some peace and quiet. When she and Monte had started dating, the chief had convinced her to become the town's coroner. It wasn't like they had a lot of nonroutine deaths, but everyone died eventually, and he needed someone to help out—and he didn't want to have to rely on someone from a bigger city nearby.

Then, there was Raelynn. She'd had to adapt to a tougher life after losing both of her parents at a relatively young age. Although the chief didn't know the depth of Raelynn's pain, he was aware that her mother has passed away from cancer and her dad had died in a tragic accident at work. She'd been so close to her father in particular, and his death had hit her hard. She was an only child, and as far as the chief knew, she didn't have any other family in these parts. Raelynn hadn't had much luck with finding a boyfriend either. That wasn't a problem—and frankly wasn't his business—but he'd also noticed that Raelynn's drinking had become worse in recent months. She never came into work impaired or noticeably intoxicated, but her work had been slacking a bit. If she didn't get a handle on this, she would be put at the bottom of his list for the chief's position.

Before he knew it, the chief was parked in front of the station. His mind was in another world with everything going on around him. Stuff even others didn't know about yet. He took a few minutes sitting inside his patrol car and stared at the entrance to the police station. He sure would miss this place.

Finally, with a huff, the chief opened his cruiser door and approached the front door. He moseyed to his office and was unsurprised to see the light flashing on his phone. He sat down at his desk and checked his messages. There were multiple from the local newspaper and television crew. So far, the investigation had stalled, and they certainly weren't at the stage to notify anyone of a possible suspect yet. That meant they had nothing to report to the media. They could wait for their big scoop. He and his officers had a more important job to do.

After debating what to focus on next, the chief decided to go through the previous day's mail. The stack had been put on his desk by the evening shift staff. Snagging the letter opener, he slid it under the flap of each envelope, carefully making his way through the pile. As he reached the bottom of the stack, an envelope caught his attention. He picked it up gingerly, like it was a delicate flower. He slowly glanced around the station, wondering if anyone was paying attention to him. Then, he pulled the letter out and opened it to take a peek. With a crestfallen expression, the chief looked over the paper in his hand. He had been expecting this—he just was not ready for its arrival.

Quite abruptly, the chief was brought back to reality as his phone began to ring. "Seneca Rocks Police Chief," he answered as he stuffed the letter into a desk drawer.

Within moments, a deep furrow was etched into his forehead as he tried to comprehend what was being said to him over the phone. By the end of the call, the chief was gripped with a dreadful sense of déjà vu. After grunting goodbye and hanging up, he glanced up and scoped out the squad room. It was going to be another long day.

CHAPTER
24

"**W**here are you?"

It was the chief. This probably wasn't a good call. Fighting against the fog of sleep, Raelynn looked at the clock on her nightstand. Oh no—she had overslept! Unable to believe her mistake right in the middle of an important investigation, she threw back the covers and sat up, except it was a little too fast and the room spun around her. She shook her head, trying to get the cobwebs out and focus on what the chief was telling her.

"Sorry, Chief! I'm heading out right now," Raelynn stammered as she hurriedly pulled on a pair of pants that had been laying in a crumped heap on the floor.

"Look, we can talk about what's going on with you later. Right now, I need you to get over to the quarry. Another body has been found. You're in charge of this investigation, and I have a funny suspicion this one is related. I've also called Monte to meet up with you. He was just getting ready to take a nap, but he said he'd be on his way."

Not another one, Raelynn thought as she hung up the phone. Maybe they weren't connected, but it seemed unlikely. After all, suspicious deaths were extremely rare in Seneca Rocks, and now they were dealing with two in a row. Plus, from Chief Austin's tone of voice, Raelynn knew this couldn't be a coincidence.

Barely taking the time for basic hygiene, Raelynn seized the rest of her clothes and gun belt and grabbed a cup of coffee. At least her automatic coffeepot was on time this morning. It looked like she was going to be working late again.

The ride into the quarry seemed to take forever. During the drive, Raelynn's mind drifted back to that day in college when she'd gotten a call that her father had been in an accident. She had spent a lot of time in that quarry with her dad. He had raised her after her mom passed away. Even though Raelynn was an only child and it was just the two of them at that point, her dad didn't spoil her. Instead, he taught her to be a strong, independent woman. In their spare time, Raelynn and her father would travel around the county, getting rid of nuisance groundhogs for farmers. Even when they were just sitting at home, watching TV, she enjoyed spending the time with him. Never did she think she would end up as an orphan.

At the time, her dad was the quarry lead, which meant he was in charge of scheduling blasting and everything that went with it. He was showing his new apprentice the appropriate way to wire a fuse. This wasn't difficult, but her father wasn't far enough away when the apprentice lit the fuse. The blast blew her father over one hundred yards across the quarry. Emergency services got there as fast as they could and tried to keep him stable until they got to the hospital. By that point, Raelynn had been notified, and she'd raced to the hospital to be by his side. When she walked in, her father was hooked up to all these machines with tubes going into his body. The doctor said there was too much internal damage. The blast had basically caused his organs to turn to mush. They were just keeping him alive until she got there.

The doctor and nurses left his room to give Raelynn some privacy and time to be with her dad. She stood at the end of his bed and cried. She didn't want to remember him in such a state. She wanted to remember him as the one who had taught her how to ride a horse and drive a car. Certain her dad would not want to stay like this, Raelynn made the hardest decision of her life: to let her dad go. She had largely avoided the quarry since the day her dad had passed away. Now, she was forced to face the hardest time of her life as she was called to enter the quarry once again for the second time in a row.

The rough gravel road at the entrance to quarry brought Raelynn out of her memories. One errant tear dripped off her chin, and she absently wiped her face with the back of her hand. She kept driving through the twists and turns of the gravel quarry, seemingly being chased by a thick cloud of dust following in her wake. When she saw a lonely guy dressed in fluorescent yellow standing over something on the ground, she figured she was in the right spot. Careful to avoid contaminating the crime scene, Raelynn parked a good several yards away from him. Then, she took in her surroundings as she walked to man.

"Detective Bailey," she briskly introduced herself. "You are?"

"William. I called it in," responded the young man. Raelynn thought he looked familiar, and apparently the man recognized her as well. "Are you Mr. Bailey's daughter? He trained me. I was there when he got blown up. I mean got hurt. Sorry." William's face promptly turned a deep plum color, and he started stuttering in embarrassment. He wasn't the apprentice at the time of her father's accident. That poor gent had moved out of the county—not that she necessarily blamed him for her father's death, but he blamed himself.

"Yes, I'm his daughter," she replied in a clipped voice. "So tell me how you came across the body." Raelynn wanted to take the focus off of her father and put it back on why she was there. While waiting for his answer, she strode around the body, eyes flitting over every detail. Raelynn's heart sank as she instantly saw the familiarity between this girl and Kate.

"I came out here after I got to work to check the quarry yard before I started setting my charges. We were scheduled to blow a new section today. I was driving up from the scale house, and I saw something lying out here. So I parked my truck over there by the loading chute and walked over to see what it was. I would never have guessed it would be a body." His voice faltered and faded on the last word. William gestured toward his truck parked by the loading chute as he spoke. The loading chute was a portable one that was moved around to various parts of the quarry, depending on where the blasting occurred. Raelynn assumed they were blasting on the far side of quarry since the loading chute was a substantial distance away.

Raelynn glanced up at William. His face was a bit washed out. "You feel okay, William?" she asked out of concern.

"Actually, not really." He wobbled slightly on his feet.

"Maybe you should go over there and sit down for a bit," she suggested kindly.

As William took her advice and staggered over to his parked pickup truck, Raelynn noticed another vehicle approaching.

Moments later, Monte pulled up in his cruiser and got out. He had a roll of crime scene tape in his hand and started putting up a perimeter without even being told to. That's what years of service on the police force did.

In the meantime, Raelynn was looking over the body and taking notes. She couldn't identify the victim yet because her hair was covering her face, and she didn't dare disturb anything at that point. From what she could tell, it was a female in her late twenties. She was wearing red lingerie too, although it was different from Kate's. There were also red rose petals around the body.

When Monte ambled over, Raelynn looked up at him. "Same pattern as before, Monte," she stated, sliding on gloves to protect the crime scene. Now, it was time to document everything. Monte had his camera with him and was ready to start capturing photos upon her say so.

"Why don't you grab some general photos before we start moving evidence," she said to him. As she resumed her task, she could hear the snapping of the shutter as he walked around the crime scene and recorded everything in film.

"Okay, ready for some closeups when you are," Monte said a few minutes later. Needing no further prodding, Raelynn bent down close to the victim's head and gently moved the dark hair that was covering her face. She almost fell back in shock when she caught sight of the face attached to the body.

"Oh, wow," Raelynn exclaimed. "Do you know who this is, Monte?"

Raelynn didn't expect him to reply in the affirmative, but he surprised her. "I do. That's the new girl in town," Monte promptly responded.

Abby Jones, the same one Raelynn had interviewed and who had discounted Thomas's alibi. What was her luck? "How do you know that?" Raelynn was genuinely interested.

"It's a small town. You tend to notice someone new."

Raelynn pondered his response while they continued to take pictures and document evidence found on the body. She knew Monte was a man of few words, but she thought he seemed to be evading her question. She would delve into that later. Right now, she had another crime to solve.

Raelynn stuck around until Darla showed up to retrieve the body. By the time she arrived, the air was starting to get stagnant, and the day had become uncomfortably warm. Abby's body wasn't in full rigor mortis yet. This told Raelynn that her death had probably happened not so long ago.

As Darla was placing Abby in a body bag, she turned to Raelynn. "Do you think this is the same person?"

Of course, Raelynn wanted to be absolutely positive before publicly stating this, but all evidence was pointing to the same person committing the crimes. That person, in her opinion, was likely Mr. Thomas Ball. In response, Raelynn said nothing—just sighed.

Darla shook her head sadly and finished up with her task. "I'll give you a call once I complete the autopsy." With that, Darla put Abby's body in the ambulance and left.

Exhausted and desperate for some time to herself, Raelynn returned to her cruiser and told Monte to head home. She wanted to sit there for a bit and ponder the possibilities. At least, that's what she told Monte. Actually, Raelynn wanted to take this time to remember her dad.

Finally blessedly alone, she sat in her cruiser and looked around her. The quarry had changed quite a bit since she'd been there last. Leaning back against the headrest, she let her eyes wander over to where William's truck was parked. In all honesty, she had forgotten about him. He was sitting in his truck at the back side of the chute. Raelynn's eyes continued to scan and eventually came to rest on an object in the top right corner of the chute. Was that a camera? Could her luck on this case actually have changed?

With renewed hope and determination, Raelynn drove over to the far side of the quarry. As she approached, William glanced up. She walked up to the driver's side door and casually leaned in. By then, William had regained some color in his face, but she noticed his eyes were moist.

"Are you sure you're okay?" she inquired softly.

William tried to deliver a sideways smile toward her. "Maybe I'm the bad apple around here. Two deaths in the quarry since I started working here," he reflected in a gloomy voice.

Raelynn couldn't believe what she was hearing. William was saying he was a jinx. No way!

"Look, just because you work here doesn't mean that these deaths come back on you," she replied reasonably. He shook his head but didn't seem too convinced by her position, so she decided to get his mind off of the subject. "By the way, I was looking at the loading chute. Is that a working camera up there?"

William simply stared at her in silence for a moment. Then, after blinking twice, he answered. "Yeah, it's a working camera. I installed that after your dad's accident," he said quietly. He had a hard time looking at her when he mentioned her dad. "I check it before I come up to the quarry to blast. You know, use it as another precautionary factor."

"Did you check it before you came up today?" Raelynn asked, trying not to sound too urgent or excited.

"Yeah, I checked the live feed, but I didn't see the body until I got up here. I guess the camera doesn't reach out that far."

The feverish sense of excitement toned down several notches at that news, but she wasn't willing to give up. "Well, could we double-check?" Raelynn asked.

"Sure. The recordings are kept down at the scale house. I'll meet you down there," William said.

Raelynn couldn't figure out how these crimes were connected except for the obvious. Kate was found on a hiking trail, while Abby was found in a quarry. Seneca Rocks sat in the Monongahela National Forest. Whoever was doing this knew Kate's body may have gone unnoticed until summertime if hunters hadn't stumbled across it. Abby, on the other hand, would have been found immediately—no doubt about that. This part of the quarry was under construction and produced thousands of tons of gravel and limestone that was shipped across the nation on a daily basis. If the explosive tech hadn't found her, then a truck driver would have.

So what was the game here? There was pretty much no chance these crimes were unrelated, but despite the obvious similarities, there were some blatant differences as well. Why? She'd just have to add that to her growing list of questions associated with this investigation.

As planned, Raelynn met William at the scale house. After leading her into an office with the security system, William rewound the film to early that morning. To her extreme dismay, once she'd viewed the footage, Raelynn agreed with William. It was impossible to see where Abby was lying.

"Do me a favor and back it up further. Let's see if there's any movement at all in the quarry," she asked. He took a moment to rewind the tape. When he pushed play, the screen was dark. Raelynn glanced at the time on the screen: 0500—hours before daybreak. She and William waited and watched. He pushed a button on the remote and sped up the tape. Right before 6:00 a.m., a corner of the screen started to light up.

"Okay, go to regular speed and let's see what we have," she requested. In agonizing suspense, Raelynn watched lights appear on the screen. The camera, she realized, didn't have a light attached to it for night view. Right now, all she could make out was a set of headlights on the far edge. The image was only visible for a few seconds before black reclaimed the screen.

"Did you see that?" she asked William, leaning over him to get a closer look.

"It looked like headlights to me," he stated uncertainly.

"I agree. Do you get a lot of traffic in the quarry at that time usually?"

"Definitely not."

"Do you have any more cameras up there?" Raelynn asked.

"No, that's the only one. It's portable and stays on the loading chute. That way, we can see if anyone is messing with the equipment," William explained.

Her face fell, but she refused to be daunted. "Can I get a copy of the tape?"

"Sure, but I have to ask the tech to get it for you. We don't have access to the physical tape here. It may take a couple of days," William warned her.

"Thanks, I appreciate it. If you can think of anything else, just give me a call," she added as she handed him her business card.

While Raelynn marched back to her cruiser, she decided she was going to stop by Abby's house again since she would pass it on the way out. Maybe she could learn a little bit more about her there.

As Raelynn approached the house, she actually looked at it, paying close attention for the first time. After crossing the porch, which looked as cute and relaxing as ever, Raelynn tried the front door. In this community, it was typical for people to leave their homes unlocked. The rate of crime in Seneca Rocks wasn't high. It was a place where everyone felt safe. Her heart panged as she wondered whether Kate and Abby had felt safe before they died.

The doorknob turned easily, granting Raelynn instant access to the house. Padding through the living room, she noticed Abby didn't have a whole lot of furniture. The couch and coffee table appeared to have seen better days.

When she entered the kitchen, she saw Abby's keys and purse were on the kitchen table. Instantly curious, Raelynn unzipped her purse. It contained normal items: a wallet with her ID in it, lipstick, and a hairbrush. There were about fifty dollars in cash inside the wallet. Dissatisfied at having found nothing of evidentiary value, Raelynn set the purse down and continued looking around. Surely Abby had a phone, yet it wasn't in her purse.

Next, Raelynn wandered over to the refrigerator. In her opinion, one could tell a lot about a person by what was in their fridge. However, this proved to be a dead end. Based on Raelynn's brief evaluation, Abby had liked wine. There seemed to be several bottles being chilled, with one of them almost empty. Other than that, she found typical food, including leftover takeout.

Unimpressed, Raelynn proceeded to take a tour of the rest of the house. The bathroom yielded little information. No prescription medications and limited toiletries. The bedroom, on the other hand, was startling. Of course, there was a bed, but it seemed to tell a story of something more than just sleeping. The pillows and covers were in disarray, and the sheets were coming off. There was little doubt in Raelynn's mind that some major activity had taken place on that bed not too long ago.

Packing that information away in the back of her mind, Raelynn opened the bedside table drawer, still on the hunt for Abby's cell phone. It contained some lotion and a pair of sunglasses. From there, Raelynn turned and opened the closet door. By her estimate, this chick was not intending to stay here long. There were only enough clothes in the closet to last her a few weeks tops. Raelynn figured she'd come to Seneca Rocks with what she could grab. Interestingly enough, there was a small hamper with some undergarments, although there were no other pieces of lingerie or anything red for that matter.

Taking into account all that Raelynn could find out about her, it seemed as if Abby had left Kentucky in a hurry. Why? What was her story? Recalling how vague and almost standoffish Abby had been when she'd come to chat with her, Raelynn walked back to the kitchen and grabbed the purse again. The least Raelynn could do was try to track down her family in Kentucky. She would also send a patrolman out to get some samples from the bed. Maybe they could get a DNA match. It would at least put someone with her at the time she died or slightly before. Plus, this could confirm one way or another whether she'd finally met up with Mr. Ball.

Raelynn secured the house and returned to her car. She put her cruiser in drive and found a country station on the radio for the ride home. She didn't want to admit it, but Seneca Rocks may just have gotten itself its first serial killer. What a horrific thought.

Drained and discouraged, Raelynn allowed her mind to retrace the events of the day. She really needed a drink after everything—the second victim, the dearth of leads, the visit to the quarry. Perhaps today would be the day that she resisted the impulse to drink away her woes. Or perhaps not. She would just have to see how she felt when she finally arrived home.

CHAPTER
25

The next morning, Raelynn went to knock on Thomas's door, but it opened right in front of her eyes. As she said hello, she realized Thomas looked like he was going on a mission. Furthermore, he didn't seem surprised to see her at his door. After a brief pause, he stepped back and welcomed her into his apartment with some apprehension.

"I guess you probably know why I'm here," Raelynn stated.

Thomas cocked his head sideways and replied, "Well, actually, no. I've already talked to you about Kate."

"That's not why I'm here, Thomas. Have you heard from Abby lately?" Raelynn inquired, closely watching Thomas's facial expressions. He seemed to smile and looked away from her.

"Well, not technically. I was just going out to see if I could find her," he replied.

"What do you mean 'find her'?" Raelynn asked, intentionally placing herself between Thomas and the front door. She didn't like the way this conversation was going. She was there to notify him of her death and ask questions before the newspaper discovered they'd found another dead girl in the area.

Right now, her theory was that Thomas Ball was the connecting link between the two deaths, and she was going to bring him in for more questioning on her turf. Although, from his response, she was starting to doubt her theory.

Thomas took a seat on his couch and indicated for Raelynn to sit as well. She waved off the invitation and remained in her authority position. The next thing she knew, Thomas had become a blubbering idiot.

"I felt really bad after Kate died, and I disconnected myself from reality," he began. Thomas was scrolling through his cell phone in his hand, and Raelynn was hesitant on letting him proceed. Should she let him tell his side of the story—again—and risk him deleting information from his phone? She decided to take the chance and let him keep rambling.

Thomas launched right into his statement without any coercion. "You see, I didn't want to deal with her death, so I turned off my phone, didn't answer messages, and stayed inside. I thought disconnecting from the world would help me get over the loss of Kate, but it just caused my thoughts to spiral out of control. I barely ate, and I definitely couldn't sleep. I hardly showered. I even became disgusted with myself. Then, today, I started thinking about Abby, so I turned my phone back on and realized I had a lot of emails from her."

Once again, he started going through his phone and paused in his story. Raelynn took the opportunity to ask a question. "Why are you so worried about Abby now?"

Thomas began to squirm on the couch, crossing and uncrossing his legs while still going through the phone. Raelynn decided it was time to seize it and make him concentrate on the conversation at hand. So she reached over and plucked it from his grasp.

He instantly went into defensive mode. "Hey, you can't do that!"

Fed up with the whole situation, Raelynn answered in a monotone manner. "I'll give it back to you once you talk to me. Now, answer my question."

Thomas stood up fast, making a break for the door. Fortunately, Raelynn had anticipated such a move and snatched his passing arm, twirling him around like a ballerina doll. With sure, practiced movements, she reached behind her back and retrieved her handcuffs, slapping them expertly on his wrists.

"What are you doing? You can't do this!"

Raelynn looked him dead in the eyes and said, "All I was coming here to do was to tell you I found Abby."

"You found her? I was leaving to find her myself when you showed up. Then, why am I in handcuffs?" Just that piece of news calmed him down, but Raelynn knew he wouldn't like the rest of what she had to tell him.

"Well, you wouldn't pay attention to me and answer my questions. Then, you tried to run, so now I'm arresting you for obstruction of justice. Maybe you will sit and listen and answer my questions down at the station," she replied.

"What questions? I don't understand what's going on," Thomas proclaimed as she led him from his apartment and down the flight of steps to her cruiser. Raelynn eyed her surroundings, thankful there weren't many folks out and about at this time of morning. She could just see the headlines on the front page of the newspaper: Seneca Rocks teacher arrested and removed from his apartment. She didn't need that attention right now.

After Raelynn placed Mr. Ball in the back seat of her cruiser, they rode in silence on the short trip to the police station. Once there, she escorted Thomas to the interview room, catching the chief's eye on her way through. She knew she would have to explain but didn't have all the evidence yet. They'd have to touch base later.

After closing the door and remotely turning on the camera, Raelynn had Thomas take a seat at the interview table. Then, she pulled out the chair across from him, taking a moment to look at Thomas and note his mannerisms. She was sure he didn't like the situation he was in.

"Have you ever been arrested before, Mr. Ball?" she asked.

"No, I've never been arrested before. I would probably lose my teaching license," he scoffed.

"The whole reason you are sitting here right now is because you wouldn't listen to me," Raelynn stated. "I asked you a question, and in your genius mind, you decided to make a break for it instead of answering."

"Yeah, since I've been sitting here, I've come to the realization that wasn't a good idea," he replied. Raelynn almost laughed at that admittance.

"So do you want to hear why I showed up at your apartment?" In a show of compassion, Raelynn got up and removed the handcuffs. She was about to deliver bad news and figured having access to his hands may help him deal with the situation.

"I just assumed it was about Kate," he stated as he rubbed his wrists where the cuffs had been. Raelynn could see he was getting impatient. She'd better hurry up and cut to the chase.

"Thomas, I came by to tell you that we found another body. It was Abby's." She paused to let the information sink in, paying close attention to his reaction. She was pretty good at reading people—that was a key skill for an officer of the law, after all. Either she was entirely off her game today, which could be a possibility after last night, or Thomas was actually shocked by the news of Abby's death. For a moment, he sat in silence with his mouth slightly ajar. Then, he slowly raised his hands to his face. They were shaking uncontrollably. Raelynn was pretty sure her star suspect was no longer her concern.

"You okay?" she asked, "Do you need something? Maybe a glass of water or some coffee?"

"Yeah, maybe some coffee," he replied faintly. Right away, Raelynn motioned to one of the day shift guys to grab some coffee. When he returned with her request, she placed the cup in front of Thomas and watched as he lifted it shakily to his lips. Raelynn noticed there were tears forming in his eyes.

"What . . . what happened to her?" he stammered. Raelynn wanted to be able to tell him something but couldn't give the case away either.

"Well, I thought maybe you could tell me," she countered.

"How could I tell you? You just told me."

"I understand that, but you see, Abby was found in similar circumstances to Kate," she divulged. The look of confusion was apparent on Thomas's face. Without a doubt in her mind, Raelynn knew he was innocent of this. God, this case was crumbling fast.

"Let's start with this," she began. "Where were you last night?" Finally, a look of comprehension passed over Thomas's face.

"Oh, I get it. You think it was me." The truth had finally dawned on him. Raelynn didn't confirm this statement. At that point, her gut told her she could dismiss him as a suspect, but she owed it to the investigation to question him further.

"Well, let's rule you out, okay?" If she tried this tactic, maybe he would be willing to cooperate with her.

"Like I said before, I hadn't heard from Abby in a while. I didn't even know she had made it to town. How could I have killed her?" he responded. At least he wasn't lawyering up—yet anyway.

"Right, I remember you saying that. Tell me why again." She thought if she could keep him talking, she may be able to figure out some missing pieces. Perhaps Thomas had some key information that he wasn't even aware he possessed.

"Look, I don't have anything to hide. I met Abby a while back online through this cooking blog. She seemed, I don't know, meek I guess." Thomas finally seemed to be in a mood to share. Glancing sideways, she saw Chief Austin watching patiently outside the interview room. She would fill him in when she was done with Thomas Ball, but right now, she didn't want to intrude on his story.

"She seemed like she craved attention—like she needed someone to talk to. At first, it was just about the recipes. Then, we exchanged email addresses. I realized I liked talking to her. It took a long time for her to tell me anything about herself . . ." His voice faltered, and he took a break, sneaking another sip of his drink. This time, he grimaced.

"Sorry about the coffee. It's definitely not the café's," Raelynn conceded. "You were saying she didn't talk much about herself. Did that eventually change?"

"Yeah. It probably was months before she finally told me about her, um, situation."

"Situation. What type of situation?"

Thomas took a deep breath before he said anything. His expression conveyed guilt, almost like he felt like he was telling on Abby. "I guess, to put it simply, it seemed like her husband was sort of holding her hostage," he finally spilled.

Raelynn sat back in her chair and crossed her arms. Abby's story kept getting stranger. She hadn't sent an officer on the errand of hunting down her next of kin yet. Maybe it would be worth her taking a trip to Kentucky.

Thomas had stopped in the story, obviously afraid to tell too much of her secret. Raelynn decided to take the lead and start asking direct questions again. "How long was Abby a hostage, as you say?" she asked.

Thomas hesitated a moment before answering, opting to finish off the contents of the squad room coffee first. "Why do you need to know? I mean, she told me that in confidence."

Raelynn nearly rolled her eyes. It wasn't like he could get her in trouble. She was dead. "Look, I need to know about her life if I'm going to find out who killed her and why. This is how police investigations work."

"So she was murdered," Thomas ascertained.

Raelynn realized she hadn't actually said Abby had been murdered when she'd told him about the death. She would give him that one. "That's what it looks like right now. At first glance, there are a lot of similarities between her and Kate's crime scenes." After sharing those details, she clammed up. She didn't want to tell him too much.

"How could Abby and Kate be connected?" he questioned. "Abby wasn't even from Seneca Rocks." Apparently, he wanted to play investigator now.

"You have a point, Thomas, but right now, they have one connection," Raelynn pointed out. "You. So, until you start talking a bit more, you are still our prime suspect." She paused and let that sink in a moment. There was no hurt in letting him think he looked good for both of these murders. After all, her gut wasn't usually wrong, but that didn't mean it was foolproof. She needed to be sure Thomas wasn't involved.

"Me?" he said in shock. "I guess you could see it that way."

"So let's get back to telling me why you shouldn't be charged for their murders," she stated. Raelynn saw small sweat beads appear on Thomas's forehead. His eyes dropped to the table, and his breathing became heavy and quick. All signs of guilt in her opinion. Maybe she shouldn't have been so hasty in her assessment of his innocence.

"Okay, okay, let me finish," he stammered. "It's true, I haven't been in touch with Abby for a little while—specifically since Kate died. I'll admit, I've taken Kate's death a little hard. I didn't think I would be affected this way. I guess my feelings for her were more intense than I wanted to believe."

"Keep going . . ."

"When I saw Kate at her funeral, I just couldn't cope. I didn't want to talk to anyone. For the most part, I stayed shut up in my apartment," he continued.

"For the most part?" Raelynn asked.

"Well, when I did decide to go out, I went over to the Rowdy Rascal bar," he admitted. "That's where I was last night actually. I stayed until last call."

Raelynn knew that would be easy to verify. One of the new officers loved setting up a checkpoint on the weekends. He got off on pulling over guys coming from the Rowdy Rascal.

"Honestly, I just turned on my cell phone this morning and checked my emails. I had a lot from Abby and realized that she'd made it to Seneca Rocks. So I was going to drive around and see if anyone had run into her," he rambled on.

"Okay, let's step back for a second. Tell me more about Abby being held hostage," Raelynn requested.

"I only know what she told me. I guess she had been with her husband for quite a while. He could get obsessive about her. She said that she couldn't leave the house unless he was with her, and he limited her access to talking with anyone. I guess he wasn't too smart about the internet though, since that's how we met," he explained.

"And you've never met her in person before?" Raelynn asked.

"No, never. I actually haven't even seen a picture of her. Honestly, I felt like she used our conversations as a way to mentally escape her environment," he said. "I never believed she would actually *physically* escape it."

"So when you said you were going to go out today and find her, how exactly were you going to do that? Especially since you didn't know what she looked like."

Thomas sort of half chuckled. "You know, I didn't even think about that. I just felt that I needed to find her," he said.

"Too bad you hadn't looked at your phone sooner. Maybe she would still be alive." That accusation should make him think about his actions. Raelynn got up from the table and walked to the door but turned back to him before leaving the room. "You're free to go," she stated. "Don't go far in case I have any other questions."

With a look of disbelief, Thomas got to his feet and nodded his head at her on the way out of the interview room. Raelynn wasn't worried about Thomas needing a ride home. Seneca Rocks was so small he could walk back to his apartment. Without a second look back, Thomas hurried out of the police station.

Immediately after exiting the interview room, Raelynn walked into Chief Austin's office. She could tell from the look on his face that he wasn't happy to have seen Mr. Ball walk out a free man. Right now, she had no other suspects and didn't have much to report until she got back some results on the evidence that had been collected.

"That looked like it didn't go the way you expected," the chief prompted, raising his eyebrows expectantly. He was nonchalantly leaning back in his chair with his hands in a praying position in front of his face.

"Well, let's just say this. I'm pretty sure he didn't kill Kate or Abby," she replied.

"So who did?" That was the question everyone was asking.

CHAPTER
26

Nate had known that Abby would leave him. It was only a matter of time. Since he had let her get the internet, she had become more brazen around him. Not only would she wear light makeup when they went out together, but she'd also think of ways to get some alone time to herself when they did go out in public.

Nate didn't kid himself about his motivations—he wanted total control of her. He'd known from the moment they started dating he wanted her totally to himself. Nate had been raised by a single mother. Not that this was unusual, but Nate had witnessed the number of gentleman callers that his mother entertained while he was growing up. Some of them were nice to Nate, while others thought he was a nuisance. Nate spent a lot of time alone while his mother tried to find a man suitable to be his father. At least that's what she told Nate.

Eventually, his mother found the perfect man to join their family. He was a widower from the neighboring town of Pike. Nate was just entering high school when this man officially moved into the house. To his delight, Nate thought very highly of him! His new stepfather showed compassion toward his mother and took Nate under his wing. In fact, he frequently took Nate fishing and taught him to play the harmonica.

A car salesman by trade, his stepfather would have to travel out of state every so often to pick up special requested vehicles. Nate soon found out that his mother took advantage of the situation when his new stepfather was out of town. It didn't start right away, but about six months into the newly formed family dynamic, Nate caught his mom cheating. His heart sank. How could any woman betray such a great man? He would sit and contemplate this for hours. Meanwhile, his mother's actions never stopped. Each time his stepfather left town, a new soul could be found keeping his side of the bed warm.

Nate's hatred of his mother's actions only amplified over time. He never told his stepfather what his mother did when he wasn't around, but Nate was determined never to let that happen to him. So when he met Abby, he knew he would never give her the chance to even look at someone else. He kept tabs on her night and day. You are supposed to be devoted to your spouse, and he was going to make sure Abby did just that.

He knew he would have to officially divorce Abby at some point, but that would come later. At the moment, he didn't even have a clue where she had gone. Abby didn't have many friends, and those she did have lived around the area. But she was too smart to stay close where he could just roll up and bring her back. No, in all likelihood, she had holed up with her secret internet boyfriend. The thing was... he had no idea how to find the guy. The son of a bitch had never specifically mentioned his address in all their communications, which Nate had carefully perused while enduring varying levels of fury.

Nate had just cracked open a beer when someone knocked on his front door. He highly doubted it was Abby. Setting his drink on the side table, he sauntered over to the door, unlocked it, and opened it a few inches. Standing on his front porch was a woman he'd never seen before. At first glance, he would say she definitely wasn't from around these parts.

"Can I help you?" Nate asked as he continued to drink in the image of the woman on his front porch. In his opinion, she wasn't bad to look at for someone who didn't do much with themselves—no makeup with her hair pulled up in a careless ponytail. She wasn't wearing any jewelry, and the clothes she had on weren't impressive either. Still . . . he could work with this.

"Hi. Are you Nate Jones?" she asked.

"What's it to ya?" he replied. Sarcasm—that was how he rolled.

"My name is Detective Raelynn Bailey. I'm here about Abby," she began as she pulled her badge out of her pocket and held it in front of his face.

Crap, Abby must have run off and notified the cops about how he treated her. Nate hadn't expected her to be that brave. He'd figured she would just disappear, especially since she hated to draw attention to herself. "What about her?" Nate countered aggressively, folding his arms across his chest.

Raelynn tilted her head and pursed her lips. Wow, he was being very defensive. Lovely how concerned he was about his missing wife. Raelynn couldn't help but roll her eyes. "I hate to tell you this, but Abby was found a few days ago. We believe she's been murdered." To Raelynn's utter shock, the door slammed suddenly in her face. Blinking rapidly, she stood looking at the neutral green paint in awe. That wasn't how she'd expected the conversation to turn out.

Surprise fast giving way to annoyance, she raised her hand and knocked again. Although it took a few moments, the door finally cracked open but didn't move any further. Firmly grasping the doorknob, she eased the door open wide in time to see Nate shuffling to the recliner in the small living room. She took this as a sign that she was welcome to enter.

As Raelynn took the first few steps into the small house, she had the opportunity to take in her surroundings. The home was quaint and definitely had a woman's touch; however, it was apparent that woman had been absent for a little while at least. Raelynn's keen eye found that the place hadn't been dusted or tidied up in several days. Pair that observation with the multitude of beer cans that covered the small coffee table, and it was obvious that Nate didn't know how to take care of himself.

Perching on the edge of the worn couch, Raelynn remained silent for a few moments, giving Nate time to comprehend the situation. Meanwhile, he sat in his recliner with his head in his hands. He honestly did love Abby. He just wanted her to only be his. That's why he guessed he treated her like he did. Maybe he didn't know how to express his love in the best way, but that didn't change how he felt about her. Now she was gone?

When he looked up, Raelynn could see his eyes were moist with grief. "I have some questions, Nate. I know I just delivered a bombshell, but I need to get some information from you," Raelynn said. Nate shook his head, which she took as a sign to proceed. "When did you last see Abby?"

"Um, it's probably been a few days. Close to a week or a little more," he answered.

"Do you know where she was?" Raelynn ventured. When Nate shook his head no, she decided to fill him in. "I'm from

Seneca Rocks. It's a small community in West Virginia. Abby was staying in our town."

"Okay," was Nate's only response.

"Have you ever been there or heard of it before?" she asked.

"Can't say that I have. I've never been outside of Kentucky."

"Right," Raelynn murmured, quirking her eyebrows a bit. "Do you have any idea how she ended up in Seneca Rocks?"

"Nope."

This was one tough interview. Nate definitely didn't want to give up any information. Did he even care that his wife was dead?

"Okay . . ." Raelynn replied, doing her best to be patient. "So I guess I'm confused on how she ended up in Seneca Rocks, which is about 3-4 hours from here. What made her leave Kentucky in the first place?" Instantly, Raelynn knew she had hit a button with good ole Nate. He started to get a wee bit squirmy in his recliner.

"How would I know why she left Kentucky?" he answered defensively. Now he was playing ignorant. He grabbed the can of beer that was sitting beside him on the side table and downed it. Raelynn listened has he crunched the can down to a small frisbee and tossed it on the pile with the others.

"What do you mean you don't know? You and Abby were married, right?" she pressed, a clear ring of authority in her voice. She was getting tired of this guy's bullshit. "Look, I didn't have to come here myself. I could have sent some local officer from Kentucky that didn't know a thing about what was going on, but instead I took the time to drive here and see you myself. You could at least help me out a little."

"Of course, we were married. Been married since high school."

"So you're telling me you don't have a clue why your wife left Kentucky." It was more of a statement than a question, and her tone made it abundantly clear she was dissatisfied with the lack of useful information Nate was providing.

"Nope," he repeated. Feeling belligerent and wrong-footed, Nate refused to say anything to this woman. She had no right to know his personal business. They couldn't prove he had ever done anything to Abby.

"Okay, I'll give you time to think about it and see if you can come up with anything," Raelynn replied as she adjusted herself on the couch to express that she intended to stay until he talked. He didn't know that she had actually talked to Abby before her death and that she'd gained further information from Thomas Ball. Based on her experiences with both, she was confident she knew why Abby had run away. All she needed was some confirmation. She would be sure to circle back around to the question later.

"So exactly why are you here?" Nate asked as he glanced over her way.

"Nate, you're Abby's next of kin. I'm here to tell you that she died and that we're looking into the circumstances of her death." *Don't you even care?* Raelynn wondered, pursing her lips with distaste. Maybe he wasn't registering what had happened. Perhaps he was still in some sort of shock. "Look, Abby is the second death in Seneca Rocks in the past week. I'd like to know more about her to see if there's a connection."

"How could there be a connection? Abby wasn't even from around those parts," he said.

"That's my point. Do you know why she left Kentucky?" Raelynn asked again, conveying urgency in her tone. "It may provide us with valuable evidence to help us find who killed her."

Apparently deeply conflicted, Nate got up from the recliner and walked over to the window. As he slid the sheer curtains to one side, Raelynn could hear him inhale sharply. "She left because of me," he finally replied.

"What do you mean, Nate?" Internally, she was celebrating. It had been a challenge, but he seemed willing to open up a bit at this point. Now, she could hear his version of events and potentially corroborate the theory she'd developed based on Thomas Ball's allegations.

"Abby left because of me," he repeated. Raelynn patiently waited for him to continue. "I may not have been the greatest husband. I truly loved Abby—maybe a little too much is all." Nate sighed and sat back down in his recliner. "Trust me, I never laid a hand on her. I wouldn't have done that, but I might have been too controlling in some people's perspectives." He conveniently decided to forget the slap he had delivered on the day that Abby had disappeared from his life.

Nate looked up at Raelynn, and his face told the story. He did love her, but relationships took more than that to work. At least, that was Raelynn's understanding given she didn't have much experience in that arena.

"Do you know why she went to West Virginia in particular?" Raelynn pushed.

"Honestly, no," he replied. "I knew she would probably leave me. I mean, you can only tolerate so much control. I could see a change in her. She took an interest in cooking, which hey, I'm not complaining about getting good food. But then she got even more quiet. Withdrawn. I guess being in the house all the time just got to her."

"Did you ever hear her mention another guy by chance?" Raelynn was tense about broaching this subject. Although she had scratched Thomas Ball from her list of suspects, it didn't mean he couldn't be reinstated. Plus, maybe there was someone else other than Thomas holding her romantic interest.

"You asking me if I thought she was cheating on me?" Nate started the questioning now, his voice gruff and assertive.

"Well, don't take it the wrong way, Nate. Maybe she met someone that gave her the attention she needed in a less controlling way," Raelynn baby-stepped.

"You've got to be kidding me. How could she meet another guy? She wasn't allowed to leave this house!" he exclaimed.

Raelynn had pushed a button, and she didn't like how he was responding. If she had to guess, he probably did know Abby was being unfaithful in some way and just didn't want to admit it to her. "Okay, okay, I get it," Raelynn soothed, trying to calm him down. She raised her hands in defense. This next question was going to piss him off even more, but she had to ask it. "Nate, I have to ask, where were you this week?" She took in a deep breath, waiting for him to explode. Instead, she heard him chuckle to himself.

"I figured you would ask that. I wasn't in West Virginia—that's for sure," he answered darkly.

Raelynn waited, but he made no further mention of his whereabouts. "So are you saying you were here this past week?" Man, this was like pulling teeth.

"Yep, I sure was. I work long shifts, and afterward, I would stop by the diner for my dinner. I sure didn't have time to go to West Virginia. Besides, I had no clue where Abby was until you told me," he reminded her. There was no way in hell that Nate was going to own up to knowing more than he did. He knew that Abby was technically not cheating on him, at least not physically, with anyone, but he did know who she had been talking to online. However, that was one piece of the pie that he was keeping in his back pocket for the future.

"I understand," she replied, though she still had a hunch he was holding something back. "It's just standard procedure to ask these questions. I'm going to assume that you want Abby's body to be brought back to Kentucky?"

"Yeah, I'm sure her family would appreciate that." Raelynn was glad at least he was considering her family because he sure didn't seem to give a crap about Abby.

Recognizing that she probably wouldn't get more information from Nate at that point, Raelynn decided to wrap it up. "Well, I guess I'll be on my way," she stated, getting to her feet and turning toward the door.

"You said that she was murdered, Detective Bailey?" Nate abruptly asked.

"Yeah, that's what we believe. She's the second girl who's been found in the same way."

"Can you tell . . . Well, you know, did she suffer?" he asked. That question tore at Raelynn's heart. How could someone ever answer that honestly? The look on Nate's face was that of sadness.

"I don't believe so," she finally said. Then, with one final look of compassion, she left Nate to surreptitiously wipe away the tear that had slipped down his cheek.

CHAPTER
27

Raelynn's drive back to Seneca Rocks was a long one. It was beautiful out. The days were starting to get warmer as spring approached. It had been two days since Abby's body had been discovered in the quarry and a less than a week since Kate had been found. She was frustrated with the investigation. Darla had performed Abby's autopsy, and Raelynn should have the results on her desk when she got into the office tomorrow. The list of suspects—more like the lack of suspects—was incredibly disappointing.

Raelynn needed to follow up on some loose ends. First, she planned to stop by the quarry's main station to see if William had been able to get the recording of the quarry the day that Abby was found. She wanted to look closer at the video to see if the brief shot of the vehicle would have anything to tell. Plus, she needed to look more into the flowers that had been found at the crime scenes. Yes, they seemed to be common red roses, but in a small community like Seneca Rocks, there weren't that many florists around. Maybe she could get a lead if the same person purchased red roses twice in a row.

Frankly, Raelynn was still in shock over the fact that the same heinous crime had occurred not once but twice within her protective town. Never in a million years would she have thought this could happen, let alone that she would be the one investigating. Sure, this could be a great opportunity for her career, but she would rather feel secure in knowing the people in her community were safe. It made her uneasy to realize that a killer was still prowling about, potentially planning his next victim. She just *had* to make more progress on this case. The killer needed to be caught and brought to justice.

Raelynn pulled into the quarry just as the sun was starting to set. She hoped she wasn't too late to catch William, but that concern was quickly dashed as he approached. He must have seen her pull into the lot because he met her at the driver's side.

"Hey, Detective Bailey," he greeted as he opened the door for her.

"Hi there, William. Were you able to get the video from the quarry camera for me?" she asked. Raelynn took a moment to relieve the tension in her body that resulted from the lack of information obtained from Nate and the long road trip from Kentucky. Her body ached, and she longed for one of her hot baths. But there was work to be done.

"I sure did. Plus, my technology guy was able to lighten it up for you, so you might be able to make out a few aspects of the vehicle." With a proud smile, William handed her a USB drive.

"That's great!" she exclaimed, eager to check out this potential new piece of evidence. "I really appreciate it. Give my thanks to your technology person." Gifting him with a brief grin, Raelynn shook William's hand and then headed back to her cruiser. She couldn't wait to see if she could possibly get a make and model of the vehicle in the quarry. That would be huge. Without a doubt, it would put her one step closer to identifying the killer.

"Okay . . . One more stop before I head home," Raelynn murmured to herself as she plopped into the driver's seat. It only took her a few minutes to reach the local florist shop, but she tried to maintain her optimism the entire ride. She had to find this guy. Kate and Abby deserved that.

A little bell tinkled above Raelynn's head as she entered the quaint little shop. Her eyes passed over the baskets of greenery, pots of plants, and arrangements of flowers lining the walls and finally landed on the graphic stating "Landry's Florist" in elegant black text. Two crimson roses intertwined to create a vibrant logo. *Ironic*, Raelynn thought to herself, eyeing the blood-red flowers.

"Can I help you?"

Raelynn swiftly turned to see a petite red-haired woman wearing a red apron enter through a door behind the counter.

"I sure hope so. I was wondering if you could tell me about any unusual purchases of red roses lately." Raelynn gazed expectantly at the woman, hoping against hope to learn something useful.

"Hmm, red roses? Those are pretty popular selections. No orders really stand out."

"Ah, hell," Raelynn muttered under her breath, too quiet for the florist to hear. "Well," she continued, thinking fast. "I'm sure it's pretty common for people to get entire arrangements of red roses. Has anyone ordered a single rose?"

"Oh, gosh," replied the florist, rubbing her forehead thoughtfully. "Maybe? I'm so sorry I'm not being more helpful.

I don't pay that much attention most of the time, and we don't keep very good records in all honesty. But for what it's worth, Chief Austin picks up a single rose for his wife every week. Isn't that the sweetest thing you've ever heard?"

Well, that's a dead end, thought Raelynn dejectedly. "Sure . . . Very sweet. Well, thanks anyway."

"No problem! Come on back if you ever need any flowers yourself."

Raelynn nodded distractedly as she hastened out of the shop, eager to get home. This avenue of investigation had been a dud, but she wasn't willing to give up yet. She simply couldn't.

Once back at her house, Raelynn locked her cruiser, emptied the mailbox, and unlocked her front door, tossing the mail unopened on the entrance table. As she walked down the hall to the kitchen, she stepped out of her shoes and took off her gun belt. Then, she made a beeline for the fridge and opened the door, noting there was very little in there. Definitely not enough to make dinner. Ignoring the voice in her head nagging at her to make better choices for herself, she grabbed a beer and sauntered into the living room.

As she popped the lid, she sat down on the couch, ready to look again at the pictures of Kate's crime scene. She was sure she was missing something. She could feel it. A new sense of determination washing over her, Raelynn placed her beer on the end table and started to rearrange the photos. Carefully, she rebuilt the crime scene like she was viewing it for the first time. Picture by picture, Raelynn recreated Kate's last day.

As she raised the cold beer bottle to her lips, she came to an abrupt stop. Haphazardly setting the beer back down, she snatched up a picture and looked at it from every angle. At the crime scene that day, she'd noticed the broken branch. She hadn't thought Monte had gotten a picture of it. Now, as she looked at the photo in her hand, she realized there were more broken branches, all pointing in the same direction as the barn. It literally looked as if sasquatch had broken through the trees in a fit of terror. She knew she was exaggerating, but it was a fair comparison considering the number of broken branches.

Since the second death had occurred, Raelynn had forgotten all about the barn. She had no idea how the barn could be connected, but it had stuck out to her for a reason. Surely there had to be *something* to it. No more excuses—this lead would be her top priority tomorrow, even if she had to hold the county clerk at gunpoint to get the information she needed.

It had been a long day, so even though it was still fairly early, Raelynn decided to turn in for the night. Before initiating her nighttime routine, she reached for her fresh beer but ultimately decided to leave it untouched. She would face the night with a clear head in hopes the dreams would subside.

True as ever to her evening ritual, she walked back to the bathtub and drew water for a bath. As the bathroom began to fill with steam from the tub, Raelynn decided that the next day would be a new day for herself and for the investigation. Filled with uncharacteristic optimism, she let herself slide into the warm water and relax. Typically, she would fall asleep in the tub after finishing her beer, a routine she had maintained since her father's death. Tonight, she would face the dreams without her beer as backup. It was a little scary—but it sure felt good.

CHAPTER
28

Chief Austin walked into the squad room feeling distracted and preoccupied. Just a few days ago, he had been sure he wouldn't need to determine a successor for a while, but things had changed. As a result, he was going to have to make a decision about his replacement sooner rather than later.

He'd purposely had the letter delivered to the police department to keep the information from his wife as long as he could. He'd thought he had more time, but the letter proved him wrong. The chief hadn't felt well for quite a while. Of course, he'd attributed it to getting older since he was approaching sixty, but a couple of months ago, his appetite had begun waning on him. Carrie hadn't seemed to notice, and even if she had, he would have just brushed it off, saying that he wanted to lose a few pounds. However, he was growing concerned.

Finally, he had decided to see a doctor at the veteran's hospital. The doctor had performed a series of tests, ruling out basic conditions. The chief didn't have high blood pressure or diabetes. This was encouraging, but then, what was the problem? Ultimately, the dreadful truth had been revealed. He'd received a letter from his doctor diagnosing him with stage two cancer. It wasn't like the chief was oblivious to the situation. He knew that there was a decent chance he wouldn't survive, and it would be hard for Carrie to cope without him. But he had to fight it if he could.

The doctor had suggested starting with a few chemotherapy treatments, which he knew would make him too sick to remain on duty. So it was time to make a decision. Unfortunately, he was still unsure about who to appoint as his replacement, especially in the middle of a critical ongoing investigation.

The chief picked up his office phone and placed a call to one of his friends. He needed some advice and knew that this person would be able to provide the perfect solution. After receiving a recommendation from his friend, the chief placed a call to the local detachment of the West Virginia State Police. Although Seneca Rocks had jurisdiction in these investigations, they could always use some help. After explaining the purpose of his call, the chief confirmed that Sergeant Riley would stop by that afternoon for a briefing. He intended to have Raelynn and Monte in the discussion because he wanted both of them to know up front what was going on. Plus, it was crucial that they understood they would have to play nice.

After getting off the phone, the chief slid the letter from the doctor into his desk drawer. He would have to tell Carrie when he got home, but until then, it was back to business as usual.

Moments later, the door to the squad room opened, and the chief glanced up as Detective Bailey walked in. After taking a double-take at Raelynn, a slow smile slid across the chief's face. Not only was Raelynn an hour early for her shift, but she had taken some extra time with her appearance. Although it was only slightly noticeable, she had added some makeup and jewelry to her typical look. Changes didn't have to be drastic to cause a meaningful transformation.

The chief motioned for Raelynn to come into his office once she got settled. He had made a pot of coffee in the squad room since the café hadn't been open yet when he'd arrived. Sick or not, even he couldn't resist the café's java and eats. Sitting back in his chair, he took a sip of coffee from the squad room and cringed. He could barely swallow. Sure, the coffee was bad enough, but the whole concept of eating and drinking was becoming harder as well.

Raelynn popped her head into the chief's office after dropping the evidence she had been reviewing on her desk. "Need some more coffee, Chief?" she offered. "I was getting ready to pour myself some."

"Nah, I'm good with this," he replied and watched her walk across the squad room with an air of confidence he hadn't noticed before. She returned with a mug full of joe and took a seat across from him.

"How'd your trip to Kentucky go?" he asked, eager for an update on this case that seemed to be stalling out.

"About how I expected, actually," she replied. "Nate wasn't too forthcoming with information. But . . . my gut tells me he didn't do this. He was a controlling and possibly downright abusive husband, but I don't think he killed Abby."

"He have an alibi?"

"Yeah, he stated he worked long shifts and then ate supper at the diner. I'm going to check it out today, but I believe him. Besides, what connection would he have with Kate? It just doesn't make sense," Raelynn explained as she raised her cup to her lips and struggled to take a sip.

"So where are you going from here?" the chief asked.

"Well, I'm going to get in touch with Darla and review the autopsy results. If Abby died in the same manner as Kate, then I would say we have a serial killer on our hands."

The chief grimaced at the thought of a serial killer. This couldn't be happening in a small town like Seneca Rocks. It was unfathomable . . . yet it seemed the only possible scenario at this point.

"You remember that old barn out near where Kate was found?" Raelynn asked the chief. Without realizing it, she slid to the edge of her seat while relaying her thoughts.

"A little. I mean, I remember you mentioning there was a barn out there, but what significance does it have in this case?" He was genuinely perplexed by the direction the conversation was going, but he trusted Raelynn and wanted her to follow her gut if it was leading her somewhere potentially promising.

"Well, maybe none, but I was looking over Kate's crime scene photos last night. There were more broken tree limbs that Monte captured in the photos."

"And? What does that have to do with the barn?" the chief asked, sounding somewhat skeptical of where Raelynn was going with this theory. He loved playing devil's advocate with his officers. He wanted them to be able to think outside the box and not get stuck on the same old theories, but as far as he could tell, this one may be pushing it a bit.

"The branches were broken in the direction of the old barn. What if that is where Kate's body came from? Somehow, she got to the middle of the trail. The barn isn't too far away from there. I didn't see any tire tracks, so the perp would have had to carry her. She didn't weigh a lot, but he would have had to go through that patch of trees to place her body on the trail. It looks like he may have gotten snagged in the process. So that's something I'm going to check into more. The barn. On day one, I went over to the clerk's office to find out who owns it, but I've never seen the results. They probably forgot about it. It was sort of a weird request."

Raelynn knew she was rambling, desperate for the chief to take her theory seriously because she really felt she was onto something. Luckily, the chief sat and listened, looking a bit dubious but open to what she had to say. "Maybe the barn is where he assaulted Kate. Then, he just carried her up to the trail and left her," she concluded.

"So do you think Abby was assaulted in the barn too?" the chief asked.

Raelynn shook her head. "No, I think that occurred at the place where she was staying. There were signs that someone had been tied up in her bedroom."

"If that's the case," the chief started, clearly warming up to the theory, "he doesn't travel far to dispose of the bodies. It's almost like he picks a quick dumpsite."

"Right. I need to go back to look at the barn," Raelynn was saying as she prepared to get up and leave the chief's office.

Back? She shouldn't have visited the barn in the first place, but the chief would let it slide ... for now. "Raelynn, you don't have enough probable cause right now to go out there. It may be easier to identify the owner and get their permission. I don't want you to stumble upon an initial crime scene and then have everything you find get thrown out of the case because you weren't supposed to be there in the first place," he warned. Then, he took a fortifying breath and continued. "I know you're in a hurry but sit back down. I need to talk to you about something."

Raelynn sat, eyes wide. She didn't like the look on the chief's face. "Everything okay, Chief?"

"Actually, not really. I wanted to talk to you and Monte together, but it looks like I'll have to catch him later," the chief replied, scratching his neck awkwardly. "I've been thinking about retirement for quite some time. You know, the boys are in college, and now would be a good time to focus on enjoying life with Carrie."

"Chief, if you think you're ready, then I'll support you," she answered, crinkling her brow in concern. It was evident there was more to this story, and she wanted the chief to know she had his back no matter what.

"Well, I appreciate that. I actually wanted to wait until we closed this case, but something has come up. I want you to know that you are one of my choices to be my replacement," he stated.

Raelynn sat back in her chair, stunned. He potentially wanted her to be the next chief of the department? Then, the full meaning of his message sank in. "Wait, one of your choices? I guess Monte is a candidate too," she surmised.

"Right. You each have different skillsets to bring to the position. I will recommend both of you to the mayor, and he will have final say on my replacement. In the meantime, I'm going to be taking some personal time prior to my actual retirement. Since I'm not going to be around to oversee the investigation, I've asked the state police to assist."

"What? You don't think I can handle this?" Raelynn demanded, instantly defensive. Impulsively, she jumped to her feet.

"Now, that's not what I said," the chief responded, motioning for her to cool her jets and sit back down. "I want someone available for you to bounce ideas off of. Someone who can provide guidance. The state police aren't taking over the case at all. I've talked it through with the colonel, and he suggested Sergeant Riley to assist. The sergeant will be here this afternoon to get briefed on the investigation."

Although she could understand the chief's basic reasoning, how could Raelynn not take this as an insult? She'd been working on this investigation since the beginning. Now, a superior was coming in from outside the department to oversee it!

"Fine, I'll try to play nice," she said waspishly.

The chief raised his eyebrows at her less-than-professional tone but decided to let it slide. "Thanks. That's all I'm asking." With that, the chief dismissed her with a simple head nod. He could tell she was fuming from the news. In fact, she was more upset about the help with the investigation than he'd anticipated. Well, tough luck. He had other things to worry about.

Taking another deep breath, Chief Austin reclined back in his chair, glancing fondly at his surroundings. He sure was going to miss this place.

CHAPTER
29

Raelynn was furious—so furious that she forgot all about the recommendation to the chief's position. With quite a bit more vigor than was necessary, she threw her empty coffee cup in the trash and snatched up her files. She had work to do before Sergeant Riley showed up this afternoon. Sitting here wasn't going to solve the case. God, she hoped that Sergeant Riley wouldn't find her incompetent and remove her from the investigation. She'd spent a lot of man hours on this case and wasn't about to give it up to the state police. She needed to follow up on some loose ends anyway, so she headed out the door on the path to find some answers.

Still driven by a sense of fury, Raelynn hopped into her squad car and slammed the door behind her. Before putting the car into drive, she took long, deep breaths, attempting to cool her rage. She knew she needed to calm down and get her head back in the game before making any investigative moves. Once she felt a little more like herself, she put the car in reverse and backed out onto the highway. Two places were on her list to visit this morning: Darla's and the clerk's office.

During the drive to Darla and Monte's home, Raelynn managed to settle down a bit. The days were starting to get warmer, and wildflowers were almost in full bloom. Eager for a distraction from her rampaging thoughts, she cracked the window to let in fresh air, instantly filling the car with the sweetness of the native flora lining the road. As she passed the café, the sweet floral scent changed to the rich aroma of coffee. She would have to stop and get her specialty on the way back through town. God knew she was going to need something to get through the briefing that afternoon.

Raelynn pulled into the driveway of the brick ranch, hoping Darla was still awake. It was early enough that Darla should have just gotten off her night shift at the hospital. After grabbing her files and walking up to the front door, Raelynn rang the doorbell. She wasn't about to tell Monte that he was a candidate for the chief's position for two reasons. First, that was the chief's news to tell him. Second, although she liked Monte, she was bound and determined to be the next chief. She was going to prove to everyone that she could solve this case and that she deserved the promotion.

After a few seconds, Darla answered the door, still wearing her scrubs. Obviously, she hadn't been home long. A smile spread across her face as she saw who was standing at her front door. Taking a step back, she cheerfully waved Raelynn in. As they walked into the living room, Darla raised her finger to her lips, indicating that Monte was asleep. Nodding her understanding, Raelynn took a seat on the oversized plush couch while Darla went to the kitchen and grabbed her coffee.

"You need a cup?" she quietly offered. Raelynn shook her head. Her stomach was still reeling from the coffee in the squad room.

Darla made herself comfortable on the couch beside Raelynn, who said, "I won't stay long. I know you probably want to go to bed."

"You're good. I don't work this evening, so I'll probably piddle around the house and run some errands," Darla replied. "Oh, I brought home the autopsy report. I was going to have Monte drop it off on your desk tonight." She got up and walked over to the rock fireplace where her briefcase was positioned.

As Raelynn watched Darla retrieve the report from her bag, she surveyed her surroundings, once again reminded of how much she loved Darla's house, particularly her living room. It was so comfy and inviting with the fireplace and hardwood floors. There were bursts of color with artfully placed throws and pillows. Darla also had some of her family pictures combined with local art on the fireplace mantel. Raelynn was looking at a framed picture of a building, trying to figure out why it looked familiar, when Darla placed the report on the coffee table, redirecting Raelynn's attention.

"Anything stand out to you?" she asked, flipping through the report as Darla once again snuggled up on the couch with her coffee mug.

"It looks pretty much like Kate's," she replied. "The toxicology report shows rocuronium in her system. Except the cause of death wasn't hypothermia this time." Darla paused in her explanation, causing Raelynn to stop and turn toward her.

"You going to keep me in suspense?" Raelynn asked.

Darla chuckled slightly and continued with her explanation. "She actually died from a seizure. From what I can tell, there was a higher amount of rocuronium in her system compared to Kate's. Maybe she put up more of a fight, but whatever the reason, Abby's body started to convulse, and her heart couldn't take it. Just shut down on her. She still had all the same signs of bondage just like Kate, except I would say her restraints may have been a bit tighter. The marks on her wrists were deeper than Kate's, but she hadn't been dead for as long when you found her either."

"I wonder if he thought Kate was already dead when he put her on the trail, not realizing she was alive and would freeze to death?" Raelynn was just thinking out loud.

"It's a possibility. You definitely have to be careful with the amount of rocuronium you administer to someone. He may not actually know how much to administer. It seems that Kate was administered too little and Abby too much. He was probably guessing at the time."

Nodding her head in agreement, Raelynn scooped up the pages of the report and stuck them in her folder. Then, she looked at her watch and stood up to go. By then, Darla had finished her coffee, and she placed her mug on the coffee table before walking Raelynn to the door.

"Thanks for everything," Raelynn said as she gave Darla a hug goodbye.

"It's my job," Darla replied with a smile on her face.

CHAPTER
30

As Raelynn pulled up in front of the courthouse, she put her game face on. She was on a mission to find out who owned the barn and to see if she could get permission to have a look around. If there was no connection, then she could scratch it off her list and come up with another theory. But if there was a connection...

Raelynn strode into the clerk's office and waited her turn in line. A young man, probably in his early twenties, was working behind the counter. He was sporting a handwritten name tag that said Nick. Raelynn looked around but couldn't find the lady she'd spoken to before. In the meantime, Nick took his time helping those individuals in front of her. Growing impatient, Raelynn glanced at her watch. The time was creeping up on her. It was almost noon, and she knew she should be heading back to the station. Finally, Raelynn made it to the head of line.

"Can I help you?" Nick asked.

"Hopefully, you can. I was here about a week ago and talked to a lady about getting information on some property."

"Oh, you must be talking about Ms. Parker. She was in a car accident and hasn't been able to come back to work yet. I'm her replacement," he stated with a strange ring of happiness in his voice. Well, that would explain why she hadn't received anything from the clerk's office.

"Well, then," Raelynn replied with a strained smile. "Let's see if you can help me. I'm looking for information about who owns some property outside of town. It has a barn on it."

"Do you have an address?" Nick asked.

Good question. She honestly had no idea. "Um, no," Raelynn replied. Nick looked at her with no emotion on his face.

"Seriously, you want me to get you owner information on an address you don't even have?" he asked in a condescending tone that instantly got Raelynn's hackles up. As if she weren't having a hard enough day already. "There's no way I'm going to be able to give that to you right now. It will take me a bit to look up aerial photographs and pin down the location. Here." Nick shoved a piece of paper at her. "The least you can do is draw a map of the area, anything you remember about it, and directions to the place. That will give me a starting point at least."

Tamping down her irritation, Raelynn did as instructed while Nick waited on other customers. For good measure, she wrote out the address for the house by the quarry where Abby had been found. She needed to determine who owned that property too. When she finished writing, she slid the paper across the desk to him. Maintaining his haughty demeanor, he gave it a quick glance and jotted down her contact information.

"I'll work on this when I get time. Do you want me to call you when I have figured it out?" he asked.

"I would appreciate it," Raelynn answered in a tight voice. "This is for a murder investigation, you know. I would think that would take priority. And you'll notice I do have an address for another property I need information on. I expect you to look into that as promptly as possible as well."

Not trusting herself to remain civil a moment longer, she turned to leave. If she hurried, she could still swing by and get coffee on her way to the briefing.

CHAPTER
31

Raelynn was busy wrangling her churning emotions as she walked into the police station. She knew the sergeant would be there shortly; she'd passed his cruiser in the parking lot of the café. Intent upon gathering her thoughts before going into this briefing, she headed straight for her office. She wanted to make sure she knew all the facts and would be able to answer questions to satisfaction. Plus, she didn't want to face the sergeant at the café beforehand.

A short while later, with her arms full of investigation information, Raelynn stepped out of her office and into the conference room housing three tables and several plastic chairs. It definitely wasn't a comfortable space, but it served its purpose.

Chief Austin and Sergeant Riley were already talking at the back of the room when Raelynn walked in. While she arranged the evidence and information on the front table, she took in the sight of her new case supervisor. By her estimate, he was in his late forties and fit for his age. His hair was just starting to betray wisps of gray around the temples. Although she had been determined to dislike the man, she grudgingly admitted to herself that she considered him handsome and distinguished in his green uniform. In the back of her mind, she reflected that she was glad she had taken a few extra minutes to improve her appearance today.

Sergeant Riley approached her with an outstretched hand. "Pleasure to meet you, Detective Bailey." She shook his hand, lingering just a little too long.

"Nice to meet you too," she replied casually.

He pulled out a chair and reached for a notepad. "Let's get started. Fill me in on where you are." Focused and straight to the point—that was something Raelynn could respect.

With that thought, she started at the beginning. By the time Raelynn had finished covering the facts and outlining her basic theories, it was after 4:00 p.m.

Sergeant Riley glanced at his watch. "Why don't we go grab some dinner and you can tell me your plans for the future," he said.

Raelynn was bent over the table, collecting paperwork. "Plans for the future?" she asked, a little stunned. Was he asking her out?

"Yeah, you know, for the case."

"Oh, right. Sure, I guess we could grab dinner," she stuttered as her cheeks grew rosy. "There's a diner just up the street that makes a good cheeseburger."

"Sounds good. I'll meet you there," Sergeant Riley agreed as he walked out the door.

To Raelynn's dismay, her agitation at the whole situation had evaporated almost as soon as she'd met Sergeant Riley. She had to admit that her heart had skipped a beat when he'd mentioned dinner, but she had to remember that this was a working meal. Nothing personal. He wanted to hear her theories about the investigation and what her plans were moving forward. It wasn't about her; it was about the case. She just hoped he would be open-minded about the theories she had come up with.

Raelynn put her files back in her office and stopped by the restroom before heading to the diner. Uncharacteristically concerned about her appearance, she looked at her reflection in the mirror. At least she'd picked today to start the first stage of her transformation. Even after a long day of work, she thought she still looked good with the makeup that was still in place. After a moment of contemplation, she pulled her hair out of her usual ponytail and ran her fingers through it until her brunette locks were resting loosely on her shoulders. Suddenly self-conscious, she debated pulling it back up but took the chance and left it down.

When Raelynn opened the door of the diner a little while later, she found Sergeant Riley sitting in the back booth. His hat was placed on the table, and a cup of coffee was already in front of him. Raelynn slid in across the booth and waved at the waitress.

"Hey, Raelynn. You want your usual?" the waitress asked.

"Um, no, Sally. Give us a minute," she replied awkwardly. All she needed was the sergeant to believe she lived here and didn't know how to cook for herself. "Just bring me a Coke for now. Thanks." The waitress nodded her head and went on to another table.

"So you come here a lot, huh?" Sergeant Riley asked shrewdly.

Dang it! He was already figuring her out. "I guess you could say that. It's quicker to stop in here than to make a whole meal for just one at home," she explained somewhat sheepishly.

"I understand that. I tend to do the same. So you said the burgers are good?" he asked as he looked over the menu.

"Yeah, that's usually my go-to, but honestly, anything on the menu is good. The cook here has been in the business for years, so you can't go wrong," she smiled.

When the waitress came back with Raelynn's Coke, they placed their orders. He took her advice on the burger, but she changed it up and got the chicken dumplings. Once the waitress had gathered their menus and headed back toward the kitchen, Sergeant Riley got down to business.

"So what are your thoughts on where to go from here?" he asked.

"Well, I had some theories . . ." Raelynn sounded a bit hesitant.

"Had some?" he inquired with a touch of skepticism in his eyes.

"Yeah. Unfortunately, they didn't pan out."

"Well, then, how do you think we should proceed with the case?" he asked. Now was the time for Raelynn to reveal her investigation into the old barn near where Kate's body had been found. She was still hung up on that for some reason. Raelynn took her time explaining about the relevance of the old barn while Sergeant Riley drained his coffee, listening intently with very little interruption. She finished up just about the time the waitress returned with their meals.

"Thanks," Raelynn said as the waitress turned and walked away.

"She seems friendly," Sergeant Riley mentioned. Raelynn smiled and dug into her chicken dumplings. They took a few minutes to eat their dinner in silence. All the while, Raelynn took the opportunity to size up her counterpart, unaware that he was doing the same.

"So until you find out who owns it, why don't we stake it out?" Sergeant Riley grabbed his napkin and wiped his face and hands.

"Stake out the barn?" she heard herself asking.

He shrugged. "Yeah. Why not? If you think the perp brought her up from the barn to the trail, let's set up and see if there's any movement at the barn. You said that the time of death was at night. We could camp out and see if someone shows up."

Raelynn's mind was reeling again. What was up with all this "we" stuff? She'd thought she was the one leading the investigation, and now he had inserted himself into a stakeout. Although, she had to admit his idea had merit, and she wouldn't have necessarily thought of it herself.

"I guess I can," Raelynn relented. "It could give us more information if someone shows up at night. I mean, who is typically in a barn after dark? I'll get everything in order and plan on making my way up there tomorrow night once I've had a chance to connect with Monte about it." Raelynn was careful to refer to only herself when addressing the idea of the stakeout. Just thinking about being out in the woods with Sergeant Riley made her nervous. She found him attractive but was hyperaware that he was supervising this case.

"I don't mind helping if you think you need it," he offered. Obviously, he wanted to be included, but Raelynn was still hesitant.

When the waitress stopped by and handed the duo their check, Sergeant Riley quickly grabbed the bill. "This one's on me."

Raelynn smiled and thanked him for dinner. "So I'll let you know what I find out," she said, leaving no doubt that she was not planning to invite him on the stakeout.

"I'm sure we will be seeing each other a lot," Sergeant Riley answered, extending his hand to say goodbye. Raelynn shook his hand and watched as he left the diner, got into his cruiser, and headed away from Seneca Rocks.

Raelynn slammed the door to her cruiser, trying to calm her breathing. She'd made it through dinner sitting across from him, but when she looked down, she noticed her hands were shaking. Why did this man make her feel this way? With an irritated sigh, she started the car and backed out of the parking lot, then turned left and headed toward home. Glancing at the clock on her dashboard, she gasped, unable to believe it was already eight o'clock. She'd had a long day and needed to relax in the bath.

CHAPTER
32

Raelynn stood inside her closet the next morning, lamenting the lack of color in her wardrobe. Today was day two of her appearance remake. Yesterday, she had added a touch of makeup and earrings. Today, she wanted to change up what she wore. She knew she couldn't go to the extreme yet, but she was thinking about adding some color to her usual plain attire.

After several minutes of deliberation, Raelynn selected a red long-sleeve button-up shirt with gray slacks. Then, she decided to French braid her hair and put in a pair of diamond stud earrings to go with her outfit. Feeling oddly confident, Raelynn grabbed her gun belt and strapped it on around her hips. Professional with a hint of girliness. She didn't look half bad.

As she stepped out of her house and locked the door, Raelynn glanced at her watch. Despite giving extra attention to her outfit, she still had plenty of time to stop by The Roast and grab a latte. She simply could not stand any more of the station's coffee.

While she was there, maybe she would talk to Mickey about supplying some grounds for them. She was sure all the officers would be appreciative. That could even be a point in her favor for the chief position.

Within fifteen minutes, Raelynn was pulling into the lot at The Roast. As she pushed open the door, she heard a bell ring, signaling her presence. A moment later, Mickey walked out from the back room and instantly smiled when he saw who it was.

"Hey there! You want your usual?" he asked as he swung a towel over his shoulder.

"Sounds good. What's up with the bell?" Raelynn asked.

"Ah, well, I'm short some baristas, so I figured, in the meantime, this allows me to work in the back until someone needs me up front. Speaking of which . . ." he began as he made Raelynn's latte. "I heard you had another murder," he said, watching her from the corner of his eye.

That's when Raelynn realized that the news of a murder had gotten out to the public, but apparently the identity of the victim wasn't yet common knowledge.

"You heard about that, huh?" Raelynn replied.

"Yeah. Anyone we know?" Mickey asked directly.

"Oh, well, maybe." Raelynn hedged, trying to figure out how to break the news to Mickey, not even sure she should tell him who it was at all. However, the more she thought about it, the more convinced she was that it wouldn't cause any harm.

"I don't know if you would know her. She was new in town. Her name was Abby," Raelynn finally divulged.

The shock on Mickey's face was undeniable. "You can't be serious," he uttered. "I just met her, and she asked about a job here at The Roast. She seemed like a sweet person from what I could tell."

Raelynn shook her head in reply. "We found her up in the quarry last week."

"What? I don't understand. In the quarry?" He handed Raelynn her latte, looking distracted.

"Um." Unsure how to handle this situation, Raelynn raised her latte to her lips. "We think she may be connected to Kate."

She hated bringing up Kate but didn't know how else to get him to understand the situation. Mickey walked around the bar, pulled up a stool, and took a seat, all the while avoiding eye contact with Raelynn. She couldn't imagine what he was thinking. Although Abby had never worked at The Roast, she had inquired about a job. Essentially, that meant they had two dead girls with a link to Mickey. Raelynn hadn't realized there was a connection before now, but maybe she needed to revisit The Roast and the individuals who worked there.

Pulling herself from her own investigative thoughts, Raelynn silently watched Mickey's reaction to the news she had just delivered. As he glumly raised his head and looked at Raelynn, she could tell he was distressed about the information but not overly so.

"Do you think it's the same person?" he asked.

Raelynn leaned onto the counter so the rest of the customers couldn't hear the conversation. "Yes," she murmured, not wanting to give him too much information about the case. She still needed to talk to more people who worked there. "How well did you know Abby Jones?"

Mickey sat up straighter on his stool. "Why are you asking?"

"Honestly, until you told me that Abby asked to work here, I didn't think there was a connection to The Roast. Now, I'm not too sure."

Mickey seemed to settle down after that explanation. "I don't think there is a connection. I saw Abby in here a couple of times prior to her asking for a job. She seemed to like the atmosphere and the company. One day, when I saw her at the diner, I just walked over to her and started asking questions. I was curious about her since we don't get a lot of strangers around here. She didn't give up much information other than she was new to town and looking for a job. I suggested she consider becoming a barista since we had an opening."

"Company? You mean she was in here talking to someone?" Raelynn drilled in on what seemed like a promising clue.

"Yeah, Dane and Tony occasionally stopped to chat with her. And Chief Austin sat down with her several times." Mickey paused, his forehead scrunching. He was clearly thinking hard. Meanwhile, Raelynn's eyebrows had practically gotten lost in her hairline. How had so many of her fellow officers interacted with Abby and not said anything about it? Well, Chief Austin had mentioned it, but she didn't realize he'd chatted with Abby on multiple occasions.

"Oh, and Monte came in and sat with her at least once. She seemed to enjoy his company because she was all smiles when they were talking."

Monte? He'd never said anything about meeting up with Abby in the café. It wasn't strange for Monte to check up on people in need. That was just the way he was. But it was still an interesting tidbit.

"Every so often he would stop in and grab some coffee to go," Mickey continued. "Always two cups."

"What's strange about that? He was probably taking some to Darla," Raelynn pointed out.

"Maybe . . ." replied Mickey, but he didn't seem convinced.

Okay, so Monte had been a lot closer to Abby Jones than he'd let on. Raelynn would have to ask him about it as soon as she saw him. It was certainly suspicious, but . . . this was *Monte* they were talking about. Surely, there was a reasonable explanation. Plus, the entire freaking police force seemed to have spent time with Abby to some extent. She had no idea how to process this unexpected information.

After thanking Mickey, Raelynn paid for her drink, realizing she needed to get to the station and check in with Chief Austin. She wanted to get a better picture of his retirement timeline.

Just as she was pulling the café's door open, she heard Mickey call behind her. "Hey, Raelynn!" She turned back, looking askance at him. "I forgot to tell you that you look really good today."

Raelynn beamed back at him before continuing on her way out the door. She wasn't used to getting compliments, but it was definitely something she could get accustomed to.

As Raelynn entered the squad room, the new information she'd discovered about half of her entire police department was forefront in her mind. She was so deep in thought she was unaware that Sergeant Riley was in with the chief. She was sitting at her desk and glanced up when he walked into her office.

"Hey there," Sergeant Riley greeted her.

"Oh, hi. I didn't even realize you were here."

"Yeah, I wanted to stop by and see if you got any new information." Really? He had been briefed on the case last night. It wasn't like she was Columbo and could solve a case within twenty-four hours.

"Well, not really. I was able to talk to Darla yesterday. She said that the manner of Abby's death was different from Kate's." Remembering her manners, Raelynn gestured for him to take a seat, and he promptly accepted her offer.

"So she didn't have rocuronium in her system?" he asked.

"Oh, no, she was dosed with the same substance, but Darla believes she died from a seizure. Apparently, Abby had a higher level of rocuronium in her system, which caused a seizure. Since she couldn't move, her body literally shut down," Raelynn explained.

"Interesting. So we need to narrow our search to individuals who could have access to rocuronium since that seems to be the common denominator between our victims."

"Right," she answered. Feeling a little out of sorts, Raelynn picked up her coffee, finished it off, and threw her cup away.

"So let's brainstorm for a bit," Sergeant Riley said. "Who would have access to rocuronium? It's not like you can walk into a pharmacy or pick it up over the counter."

"Right. It would have to be emergency medical personnel or individuals at the hospital."

"Did the coroner mention anything about having any missing?" he asked.

"Honestly, I never asked her," she admitted, instantly kicking herself for not thinking of that. Of course, Darla would know if any drugs were missing. "I'll reach out to her. We will have to wait until she gets back to the hospital and reviews inventory to make a move on that lead. In the meantime, I can reach out to the local emergency squad director and ask about it. I think it would be best to go through the director anyway in case the perpetrator ends up being someone who runs with the ambulance."

"That's a good idea. We don't want to show our hand," he agreed as he got up from his seat and put his hat back on. Raelynn let out a slow breath, taking in his stature. "I'll think I'll stop by The Roast and grab a cup of good coffee on my way back to his station on the other end of the county."

"Oh, yeah, sorry. If I had known you were going to be in the office today, I would have grabbed you one when I stopped," Raelynn apologized. "Speaking of . . . Mickey—he's the owner of The Roast—said that Abby had been in and they had talked about a job for her. And . . ." Raelynn motioned for him to come closer to her and whispered the next line. "Apparently she met several of the Seneca Rocks officers there a lot."

Sergeant Riley stood up a little taller, immediately understanding the possible implications of the information Raelynn had just laid out. "You think one of your comrades could be involved in this?"

"I don't know . . . I mean, I wouldn't think so, but it stuck out to me. Why didn't anyone say anything?"

"Which officers?" Sergeant Riley's voice had taken on an urgent tone. Was it her imagination, or was there a glint of concern in his eyes? Concern for . . . *her*?

"Dane, Tony, Monte, and the chief." As Raelynn spoke, she glanced all around, making sure no one could overhear their conversation. If she was on the completely wrong track, this line of questioning could get her into deep trouble.

"Raelynn," said Sergeant Riley, capturing her in his intense gaze. "This is important. Do any of those four men seem like they could have done this? I know they're your coworkers, but I am worried about who could be next. I'm worried about *you*. We need to rule all of them out."

"No! I mean, it sounded like Monte interacted with Abby the most, but . . ."

"Do you think there was something going on between the two of them?"

"Look, I'm not sure. All I know is that Mickey said Monte would come in, and they would talk. And sometimes Monte would stop by and order two cups of coffee. Mickey was certain that it was for Abby." Raelynn wrapped her arms around herself, looking doubtful and confused. "I want to believe that he is just a good guy, and since she didn't have anyone in town, he was just showing her kindness. Plus, it's hard for me to believe he would cheat on Darla. But I guess it's worth looking into that."

"Wait, what? Monte is dating Darla? The coroner?" Sergeant Riley asked.

"No, they aren't dating," Raelynn laughed. "They are married."

"So you're saying that we have an officer who is married to the coroner?" he remarked to himself. Raelynn could tell he was rolling the information around in his mind.

"Right," she confirmed, raising an eyebrow. Why was this such groundbreaking news? "I was going to ask Monte to go with me tonight and do some surveillance at the barn I mentioned to you. I also stopped by the clerk's office, and there's a new guy working. He said he would try to get me the information this week, but I'm sort of impatient." Raelynn shrugged. "I thought maybe I could ask him about Abby while we are sitting and watching. I haven't had the time to really talk to him about the investigation lately. I figured it would be a good chance to catch up."

"Well, I prefer that you don't go alone at least," Sergeant Riley said, but she could tell he was annoyed that she was going to have Monte accompany her rather than him. At least, that was what Raelynn could sense.

"Well, I'll keep you updated if I get any new information. I'm not too confident that the barn will yield much tonight, but what the heck?"

His face clouding over with a look of unease, Sergeant Riley nodded and left her office.

CHAPTER
33

Sergeant Riley swung into the driver's seat of his cruiser, unable to turn his mind off about the information Raelynn had told him about her fellow officers. He didn't know about her, but it sure did send up red flags for him. After backing out of the station's parking lot, he headed out of town. When he saw The Roast up ahead, he decided to take the opportunity to get a cup and ask a few more questions.

A bell chimed, announcing his arrival, when Sergeant Riley pushed open the door of The Roast. Glancing around the café, he noted it definitely had a warm, inviting atmosphere. There weren't many patrons in the dining area, but it was still during work hours. He figured there was more business in the mornings and evenings.

The sergeant headed to the counter and looked over the menu that hung above the bar. Before he could finish perusing the options, a gentleman with hair tips of blue emerged from the back of the café. Sergeant Riley figured this was Mickey, the owner.

"Welcome to The Roast," Mickey said as he approached the counter. "What can I get you?"

"Well, let's start with some coffee," Sergeant Riley replied.

Mickey's expression became puzzled, but he decided to focus on taking the man's order first. "Okay, what will it be?"

The sergeant stared at the menu, unsure what most of the items were. He was old school and liked just plain old black coffee. "Can I just get a cup of black coffee?"

Mickey laughed at the hesitant request. "Of course. That's actually my specialty. Do you like a strong coffee or something on the milder side?"

Although it was still a bit earlier in the morning, Sergeant Riley was afraid to get too strong of a cup and risk being up all night. "Better go on the milder side," he decided.

As Mickey got busy with his coffee request, Sergeant Riley watched in amazement, impressed at how he selected a certain coffee bean from a dispenser and processed them into smooth grounds. Next, he poured the grounds into a filter that he placed over an empty cup and expertly poured hot water onto the grounds. In an instant, Sergeant Riley was struck by the fresh aroma of high-quality ground coffee. Finally, Mickey took the filter away from the cup and placed it in front of his new customer. He'd performed the ritual in just a matter of moments, and the sergeant had to give him credit. The coffee was incredible.

"So you said you'd start with some coffee. What else can I help you with?" Mickey asked as he cleaned up.

"I'm Sergeant Riley with the state police, and I'm helping Detective Bailey with the death investigations of the two girls. She mentioned something to me today, and I thought I would just ask some follow-up questions."

"Well, I'll see if I can help you out," Mickey acquiesced, but he doubted he had anything else to add.

"Let's start with Abby," Sergeant Riley stated. "Did you know her personally?"

"Personally? No, I did not. She came in a couple of mornings, ordered a coffee, and sat at that back table." Mickey pointed to an empty booth at the far end of the café.

Following his motion, Sergeant Riley noticed the booth was sort of tucked away from the others but had a good view out a window. "Was she ever here with someone?"

"She always came in by herself and sat there for quite a while. But often, someone or another would end up joining her."

"Who? Anyone I know?"

"Well, I guess you know Chief Austin. And Monte. And the other officers would check up on her from time to time. Not sure you would be familiar with anyone else. You know, everyone's so openhearted and caring around here. A newcomer comes around, and people welcome them with open arms. It's hard to say whether anyone was paying Abby extra special attention, but she was certainly noticed. We don't see strangers here all the time." Mickey bestowed a pointed look upon Sergeant Riley, indicating that he should know since he was a newcomer himself and had been greeted by countless locals already.

"Did anyone interact with Abby more than the others? Did anyone stand out to you?" Sergeant Riley was trying to sound casual but was failing miserably.

"I don't know. I really didn't pay much mind. I'm short staffed, and mornings tend to be a busy time for me," Mickey explained regretfully.

"I can see how that would be a money-making time for you," conceded Sergeant Riley with an understanding smile. "Well, I won't take up any more of your time. Thanks for the coffee."

Still digesting all the information he'd just received, Sergeant Riley left the café and headed toward his cruiser. As he stepped out into the sun, he took a minute to look around the outside of the café. There weren't a lot of parking spots, but in a town this small, it wasn't like everyone would be at the café at one time.

Glancing across the street, he realized that someone had created a parking spot in between some trees. After looking both ways, he crossed the street and inspected the area. The grass had been crumpled by visible tire tracks. It looked like this spot was used quite frequently in the past but not so often anymore. He could see where new undergrowth was pushing up through the trampled grass. It seemed that the space had been left undisturbed for a while now, allowing grass to grow back.

Unable to shake his sense of unease, the sergeant wondered if this was where the killer would sit and wait on Kate. To a common person, he would just look like an officer trying to catch speeders. No one would suspect potential underlying reasons for parking there.

Intent upon digging up as much information as he could, Sergeant Riley walked around the area, looking for any other clues that could identify the person who consistently parked there. Unfortunately, he didn't find anything else that provided evidence one way or the other. Ultimately, he gave up his search and returned to the café parking lot.

Still behind the counter, Mickey watched as Sergeant Riley crossed the street, obviously looking for something. Then, he watched as he approached the café again. The familiar bell rang as he entered.

"One last question, Mickey, I promise," Sergeant Riley stated as he approached the counter. "Did you ever see anyone parked across the street?"

Mickey shrugged. "I guess a police officer because anyone else would probably get a ticket for loitering there. The only person who comes to mind is Monte. Typically, the other officers liked to sit close to the county line to pick up the drunks returning from the bars. But who knows?"

Sergeant Riley nodded absently and threw him a casual, "Thanks." As he was leaving the café, his radio squawked with information regarding a traffic accident. While climbing into his cruiser, he answered that he would be heading to the scene momentarily.

It took him about five minutes to arrive at the rollover accident. The ambulance was still on its way, so he walked around the vehicle to ascertain the number of victims. From what he could see, there was only a driver involved. Squatting down on the ground by the driver's window, he observed that the driver was conscious but stuck in his seatbelt. The sergeant could see some visible head trauma.

"Hey there. I'm Sergeant Riley. The ambulance is on its way. You hang tight with me. Everything's gonna be okay." The driver turned his head and gave a pained grimace.

Satisfied the man would hang on for at least a while longer, Sergeant Riley stood up. He could hear the sirens coming in the distance. He walked around the car again, trying to figure out what happened. He didn't see any skid marks, so apparently the guy hadn't hit his brakes to avoid something, such as a deer. It looked like he had just gone around the turn and forgotten to straighten back up, hitting the embankment and rolling the car. Luckily, the vehicle didn't look to be in that bad of shape. The driver hadn't hit anything as far as he could tell. He did notice that the car had Kentucky license plates, but that wasn't unusual for this area. The Kentucky border was only a few hours away, and out-of-staters tended to use this route to travel to Washington, D.C.

Sergeant Riley bent down to the window again. "Are you able to talk to answer some questions?" he asked the driver.

The man shook his head slightly.

"I see you're from Kentucky. What's your name?"

The driver took a breath before answering. "Nate Jones."

"Where you headed, Nate?"

"Seneca Rocks."

Well, he'd almost made it. Sergeant Riley stood back, allowing the EMTs to do their job. The fire truck had also arrived on scene and was preparing to cut him out of the car.

Sergeant Riley radioed for a tow truck and retreated to his cruiser to start paperwork while the emergency personnel worked on getting Nate out of the car. After almost a half hour, Nate was safely ensconced in the ambulance. When Sergeant Riley left the scene, following the ambulance to the hospital, the tow truck was loading Nate's car. He would finish up his report later. For now, he had to make sure this guy was okay. After all, that was the kind of man Sergeant Riley was—always looking out for others in his community and now in Seneca Rocks.

CHAPTER
34

Raelynn was able to get ahold of Monte later that day to ask him to accompany her on the stakeout. Before settling in for what was likely to be a very boring night, she wanted to stop by the diner and grab a burger. Nothing worse than sitting there in silence and hearing your stomach grumble.

Upon arriving at the diner, Raelynn sauntered to her normal booth and slid in with her back to the wall. There was something comfortable about the diner. The booths were covered in red leather, and the tables were adorned with containers full of sugar and powdered creamer for coffee. There weren't many customers yet, but Raelynn knew that they would be streaming in shortly.

Sally, the waitress, made her way back to Raelynn's booth. She was wearing the standard-issue uniform for the diner: black pants and a white shirt. Wrapped around her waist was an apron, which she used to hide her tips and order book. For as long as Raelynn could remember, Sally had always been a waitress at the diner. Of course, she had aged over the years, just like everyone, but Raelynn couldn't remember her looking any different than what she looked like now.

"You alone this evening, or should I be expecting your new friend?" Sally asked with a teasing smile on her face.

"Just me tonight, Sally," Raelynn replied. Instead of taking her order, the softly smiling waitress looked around the diner and slid in the booth across from Raelynn. Puzzled by Sally's unexpected action, she asked "Something up?"

"Look, I know you've been a little guarded about dating," Sally began.

"Well, I wouldn't quite say that . . ." Raelynn interrupted, unsure whether she should be offended.

"Really? When was the last time you went on a date?"

Raelynn thought about it for a moment. Dang, this answer was harder than she thought. "What's your point? So I don't get out much."

"Raelynn, honey, this whole town knows your dating habits—or lack thereof, I should say," Sally went on. "We want what's best for you. We all consider ourselves part of your family, especially since your dad passed."

Distinctly uncomfortable with the direction of the conversation, Raelynn began squirming in her seat and let her gaze transfer to the window. She knew Sally was right, but she had a hard time letting her guard down. She never had been close to anyone except her family. Plus, her job certainly didn't help. The individuals she interacted with on a day-by-day basis as a law enforcement officer weren't exactly dating material. She didn't typically see the good side of people. It wasn't like she was going to ask someone out after arresting them for public intoxication.

"I noticed you yesterday with the state trooper. Your face was lit up. I could tell you were attracted to him," Sally conveyed.

"You could tell that?" Raelynn asked, horrified. She could feel her face getting warm. If Sally had noticed, who else had noticed? Sergeant Riley? *Everyone?*

"Oh, honey, I don't think I was the only one who could tell. Maybe it's time to consider getting your life started," Sally said gently as she began to slide out of the booth. She put a hand on Raelynn's shoulder. "You want your usual?"

Torn from her moment of suspension in utter mortification, Raelynn managed to look up at Sally and smile. A thousand different thoughts about Sergeant Riley were going through her mind as she actually acknowledged what Sally had told her. "Yeah, that'd be perfect."

Within what seemed like minutes, Sally was sliding her traditional dinner of a burger and fries in front of her. Meanwhile, Raelynn had been right—more patrons were starting to arrive at the diner for suppertime. There was plenty of opportunity for people watching, but Raelynn's mind was far away from the diner.

As she ate, she repeatedly caught herself thinking about Sergeant Riley. What little time they had spent together had always been related to business. She thought she could sense there was some other connection between the two of them, but she didn't want to get her hopes up. She had a case to solve, which was her number one priority. Plus, she was just considering dipping a toe into the dating pool. It wasn't like she was looking to dive in headfirst. Nonetheless, she had to admit that Sergeant Riley had really captured her attention and wouldn't let go. With that in mind, she hoped she could make exploring the possibility of a relationship with him her number two priority.

As Raelynn pushed away her now empty plate, she looked at her watch. It was almost six o'clock in the evening. Monte was supposed to meet her at seven at the station, and they would head up to their stakeout post from there. Thinking it wouldn't hurt to arrive at the station early, Raelynn gestured at Sally to bring her the check. Then, she left her normal tip on the table and gave Sally money to cover the bill.

"Hey, Sally?" Raelynn was able to briefly snag her attention before she walked away. "Thanks for caring."

Sally waved her hand like it was something she did all the time. Raelynn nodded at familiar faces as she headed out the door. She had a big night of probably no action at all in front of her.

CHAPTER
35

It was a little after seven when Monte walked into the station carrying two cups of coffee from The Roast. Raelynn had already packed her cruiser with warm gear for their adventure tonight. In her line of work, she was naturally a little pessimistic on a daily basis, but when things panned out to her advantage, she enjoyed the accomplishment more than ever. Despite her assumption that the stakeout would yield very little information, she was hopeful that her hunch would be validated. Only one way to find out . . .

Ready to get this stakeout over and done with, Raelynn walked over to Monte and accepted the coffee he was handing to her. As her hand grasped the hot beverage, her mind went back to Mickey at The Roast stating that Monte would occasionally come in and order two cups of coffee. Here he was again buying two cups of coffee. The only difference was that she wasn't one of the dead girls.

"Ready?" he said. She nodded in response and grabbed her jacket off the back of her door as they headed out.

"I already have stuff packed in my cruiser if you just want to travel together," Raelynn offered. "I don't expect to be out there too long. Either we'll see movement, or we won't."

"Sounds good to me. I told my crew and dispatch already that I won't be able to respond right away if they try to contact me. You know, pretty much the only communication up there is by radio since it's so remote."

Walking side by side, they headed out of the station and to her cruiser. By now, the darkness was settling in. Raelynn had made it a point to look at the weather before scheduling to stake out the barn. No rain was in the forecast, and there were only a few clouds in the sky. The moon and stars were bright and emitted a faint glow to guide the way on their adventure.

It took roughly fifteen minutes to make the drive to where Kate had been found. They had debated on the way there whether they should set up facing the front of the barn or creep in from behind. Ultimately, the pair decided that behind the barn gave them the best cover. They didn't want the cruiser to be visible; that would potentially deter any illicit nighttime activity.

Once parked in their selected spot about a quarter mile away from their destination, Raelynn and Monte unloaded the items they would need. Before embarking on their short hike, she made sure she grabbed her binoculars, jacket, and coffee—clear necessities for a task such as this one.

Although it had barely been a week, the grass and weeds had grown a bit since they'd last traveled on the trail. They found themselves walking through almost knee-high undergrowth on the way to the stakeout post. The trees were no longer bare; buds were popping up on their branches as spring began to make an appearance. The air smelled so fresh. Raelynn loved being in the outdoors, and the earthy scent of nature gave her a sense of peace despite the probable tedium the night offered.

It took Raelynn's eyes some time to adjust to the increasing darkness. After several minutes, the duo stopped about one hundred yards from the back side of the barn, which sat at the bottom of the hill. This vantage point provided a good overview of the field and the barn, and they'd even be able to quickly identify any cars or people approaching the area. Settled in for the long haul, they sat and waited.

CHAPTER
36

Sergeant Riley left the hospital a little after seven in the evening. To his relief, Nate was going to be okay. According to Nate, he had been driving too fast and couldn't correct the vehicle after coming out of the turn. The crazy roads in West Virginia could take out even the best driver. If someone wasn't from the area, they definitely needed to drive the speed limit and possibly take Dramamine because motion sickness was pretty common. Most of the roads were two lanes cut into mountains. Not only that, but there were numerous distractions, such as animals, that could become hazards.

As Sergeant Riley determined after a brief but painful conversation, Nate's head hadn't been in the driving game at the time of his accident. He'd been coming to Seneca Rocks to confront Thomas Ball about Abby leaving him. After Detective Bailey had showed up at his house, Nate had determined where he could find the guy Abby had been talking to online. It wasn't hard to do a Google search and find out that Thomas Ball worked at the high school. The internet could provide a wealth of information.

But fate had derailed his plans. As Sergeant Riley discovered, Nate had been on a mission to find this Thomas Ball guy, but now he was confined to a hospital bed. No chance of him confronting his wife's online lover now. Abby was gone anyway—gone where neither Thomas nor Nate could reach her. Hopefully, Nate could find peace and move on.

Sergeant Riley was on his way home when he decided to make a quick stop at Darla and Monte's place. There probably wasn't much more Darla could add to what she had told Detective Bailey, but Sergeant Riley knew she may look at things differently if he broached the subject. Aware that they lived in a ranch house on the way to the hospital, he figured he would be able to find it by the name on the mailbox. Otherwise, he would just have to stop and ask someone. After all, everyone knew everyone in this town. Someone would be able to give him directions. As he approached each house, he slowed down to read the mailbox. It didn't take him long to find the correct place. The home was situated a little off the road, a quaint stone ranch with a garage.

As he swung into the driveway, he noticed there were a couple of lights on inside. Someone was home, and he assumed it was Darla since Monte was due to be on a stakeout with Detective Bailey. After cutting the engine, the sergeant stepped out into the dark, then made his way to the front porch and knocked on the door. He only had to wait a few moments for his knock to be answered. Standing in front of him was an attractive lady in her late thirties with her dark hair falling around her shoulders. She was clearly dressed for a comfortable evening at home, as she wore a long T-shirt over leggings.

"Hello. May I help you?" she asked politely, keeping the door mostly closed to prevent him from seeing too far inside.

"Hi, I'm Sergeant Riley with the state police. I'm sorry to be stopping by at this time of night, but I was on my way home from the hospital and wanted to talk to you real quick."

"Hospital? Is Monte okay?" She immediately opened the door wider, a look of surprise on her face. Sergeant Riley promptly shook his head, realizing that hadn't been the best lead-in for what he was there for.

"Oh, sorry! Yes, ma'am, Monte is fine. I'm so sorry for that confusion. That's on me." Darla seemed to visibly relax as the sergeant reassured her. "I do apologize for that. I'm actually here because I'm helping Detective Bailey with the murders of the two girls. I was hoping to ask you a few follow-up questions. I promise it won't take long." Charming as ever, he put up his hand in a sign of a promise.

A slight smile started to form on Darla's face. Needing no further explanation, she opened the door fully and motioned for him to come on in. "Feel free to have a seat."

"Thanks, but I'm good. Hopefully, I won't take up too much of your time. I know it's getting late," he said apologetically as he followed her into the living room. The home was modest when it came to décor. Earth tones made up the soothing color palette, creating a natural and beautiful vibe in the open space, and there was an amazing fireplace in the middle of the living room as well. "Wow, that's gorgeous!" he exclaimed, making his way over for a closer look.

"Oh, thanks! That was one of the original features of the house. It's actually what made me fall in love with this place," she stated as she took a seat on the couch.

"You have a lovely home," he said with genuine warmth.

She smiled in reply. "So what can I help you with, Sergeant Riley?" she asked.

"I hear you're married to Sergeant Monte at the police department," he began, gently initiating his tricky line of questioning.

Darla smiled fondly. "That's right. We've been married about two years now. Actually, Raelynn—I mean, Detective Bailey—introduced us."

"That's nice. Still in the newlywed stage of marriage, huh?" he responded jovially. This made Darla giggle.

"I guess you could say that," she said with a sly glance over to him. Although his words indicated he was fully engaged in their conversation, he also seemed to be taking a great interest in the photos on her fireplace mantel.

"So do you and Monte talk about cases much?" he asked as he turned back toward her.

"Sometimes, but only typically when I've been involved as the coroner. I'm very careful not to violate HIPAA when it comes to my patients," she responded. "And normally I'm not involved unless a person is dead."

"So it would be safe to say that you and Monte have talked about the two murders, right?" he inquired.

"Well, sure, but Raelynn is the lead on the case, so I've definitely discussed it more with her."

"What did Monte say to you about the case? Anything specific?" he pressed.

Instead of answering immediately, Darla took this time to look at Sergeant Riley and tipped her head. "Why are you asking me these questions, Sergeant?"

"Okay, so here's the deal," Sergeant Riley sighed, not overly enthusiastic about how the conversation was going so far. "I'm with the state police, and it's my job to find out who committed these two murders, no matter who they are. The more we investigate, the more certain members of the Seneca Rocks police force pop up. And one of those people is Monte. I know it sounds weird, but it could all be a coincidence, so I was hoping you could clarify it a bit for us."

"What do you mean by 'popping up'? I mean, he's been helping Raelynn with the case. Of course, he's going to be involved," she countered.

"Right, and I'm not suggesting he's guilty of this. I just need to explore all possibilities, and Monte has given me reason to believe he *could* be involved. For instance, we found out today that he has a connection with both of the victims."

"Other than being the first responder at the crime scenes? I just don't understand."

"It's okay," Sergeant Riley said soothingly. He hated upsetting Darla, but something about Monte was bothering him, and he needed to make sure Raelynn was safe. He'd only just met the woman, but there was no doubt in his mind she was special, and he was determined to rule out Monte before he turned his attention to Chief Austin, Dane, and Tony. "Just . . . tell me about him. What's he like? What's your marriage like?"

Clearly self-conscious, Darla pulled her legs up under her on the couch. She seemed distracted, and it took her a bit to answer. Despite his internal sense of urgency, he didn't rush her. These questions were certainly difficult to answer. It was possible that Darla hadn't realized what had been happening right in front of her and had been refusing to acknowledge it until he thrust the issue right into the spotlight.

"Our relationship isn't perfect. Whose is, right?" she began. "I work a lot of hours at the hospital, usually night shift. As you know, I'm also the county coroner, though that doesn't take up much of my time. I chose night shift because Monte's the sergeant on the night shift, and this arrangement works for us. We're able to have some time together before we go to work. And he visits me at the hospital whenever he can. He's a very caring husband."

Sergeant Riley latched onto that comment. "Tell me about his visits to the hospital. Was he on duty when he came in, or was it usually a surprise visit?"

"Oh, he was usually on duty. He would come in for car accidents, fights, and such. He does come in randomly though when he isn't working. I've found him wandering around in the ER or waiting for me down in autopsy."

"Do you think he could have access to rocuronium?" Sergeant Riley asked point blank. Struck dumb, Darla sat there in stark silence. The sergeant carefully watched her reaction. Apparently deep in thought, she took another long moment before slowly lifting her head to meet his gaze. He wasn't sure, but he thought he could see tears starting to form in her eyes.

"Oh my god." She lifted her hands to cover her face. "How come I didn't think about this before?"

"Look, it's just a theory. We've found he has some connections with Kate and Abby. There are just some unanswered questions is all." Sergeant Riley wanted to set her mind at ease, but at that moment, she got up from the couch and started pacing the floor.

"What type of connections between the girls? I thought Abby was new in town," she murmured, wringing her hands restlessly. Sergeant Riley hesitated, unsure how much he should divulge, but he thought she had a right to know the facts they'd gathered at this point. The more information she had, the more likely it was that she would remember some behavior changes in Monte. He wanted them to work together to connect the dots.

"Well, apparently, he would sit across the street from The Roast and wait on Kate to get off work."

Darla stopped in her tracks and turned to look at him. "You're telling me that he and Kate were having an affair?"

Sergeant Riley took a few steps toward her. "Look, I don't know for sure. We don't know the nature of their relationship at this juncture." He tried to sound reassuring to Darla, but she looked anything but reassured.

Unmistakably agitated, she began running her hands through her hair and down her face. Finally, she sat back down on the couch. "Tell me about Abby," she commanded.

"Well, she started visiting The Roast in the mornings. He would come in and sit with her. Of course, he wasn't the only one to visit with her. Apparently, all of Seneca Rocks wanted to befriend the new girl in town." As he spoke, Sergeant Riley turned and surveyed the pictures on the mantle of the fireplace again. He remained quiet for a while after finishing his explanation, letting the information sink in for Darla.

"So you're telling me that he started seeing Abby too?" she eventually inquired.

Sergeant Riley barely heard her question. A photo on the mantel had snared his attention. "Um, sorry. This is an interesting picture. Is it local?"

Darla looked up to see him examining the photo of her old family property. "Yeah, it's been in my family for years."

As she spoke, Sergeant Riley pulled the photo out of the frame and flipped it over. Written in elegant cursive on the back was an address. Bingo.

But his heart had plummeted the moment he'd caught sight of the structure, so familiar even though he'd never seen it before—only heard it described by the woman he hadn't been able to get out of his mind for the past twenty-four hours.

Without a word to Darla, the photograph still clutched in his hand, he grabbed the doorknob and let himself out of the house. After sprinting to his cruiser, leaving Darla dumbfounded on the doorstep, Sergeant Riley jumped in, put the car into reverse, and backed out onto the roadway without evening looking. Then, he put his lights and sirens on and sped through the town to the outskirts of the Monongahela National Forest.

CHAPTER
37

Raelynn was getting antsy. Waiting wasn't her strong suit. When she glanced over at Monte, she noted he seemed to be restless as well. Stakeouts . . . Whose dumb idea had this been again?

"What do you say we just walk around the outside of the barn?" Raelynn suggested as she got up and started down the hill. She figured Monte would follow without much problem. Sure enough, when she glanced behind her, she saw Monte get up without argument.

Raelynn's eyes had adjusted to the dark, and her other senses had sharpened as well. She could hear the faint sound of the wind whispering through the trees; smell the soap that Monte had used in the shower before starting his shift—it had a slightly piney aroma; and hear the crunch of the tall grass under their shoes, each step announcing their arrival as they got closer to the barn.

Uncharacteristically nervous, Raelynn tried to control her breathing. She wanted to make sure that she stayed calm in order to absorb any clues or evidence the environment might present to them. Monte was close behind, following in her footsteps, but after a while, she stopped briefly to assess her surroundings. They stood still; it was like they were sneaking up on their prey.

Raelynn took a deep breath. They were about one hundred yards from the barn, and she could feel her heart start to speed up. After taking two steps forward, she sensed something wrong a split second before it happened. A low cry coming from Monte shattered the suddenly tense silence. Then, a blow hit her without any other warning, knocking her off her feet. As she landed in the grass, the sky began to spin around her. The last thing she saw before she passed out was a face filling her vision. Then, all was black.

CHAPTER
38

Raelynn's eyes seemed so heavy. She couldn't get them to stay open, no matter how hard she tried. Willing her brain to cooperate, she fought her eyelids, painfully prying them open. A dim light penetrated the darkness, but the barely discernible glow hurt her head, so she promptly squeezed her eyes shut again. Raelynn couldn't remember what had happened, but she could feel tremendous pain in the back of her head.

Severely disoriented, she tried to lift her hand, but something was preventing her. Alarmed, Raelynn turned her head slowly to the left and felt pain radiate down her neck. On top of that, she could feel her heartbeat pounding in her temples. After taking a couple of breaths to relax, she slowly opened her eyes. While the blurriness gradually cleared, she continued concentrating on her breathing. She knew unless she was in control of her own body, she could not control anything else.

As her vision finally came into focus, she could see that she was inside of a building. She thought she could see small bugs flying through the air. It seemed there were thousands of them. She had to be hallucinating, right? The light was not bright, and she couldn't make out much, but she kept blinking in an effort to get her eyes to focus more. She couldn't concentrate with the pain in her head. Every time she tried to move, even just a little bit, the pain would explode, causing her to retreat back into the darkness. She had no concept of how long she lay in the black abyss.

Like a tiny candle being lit, Raelynn's consciousness flickered back. She felt like she had been lying there for hours. The rest of her body had succumbed to aches and pains. Before she opened her eyes, her other senses started to take over. She could hear quiet breathing and a slight shuffling across the floor. Cold dread washed over her as she realized there was at least one person there with her. Afraid to move, she lay as still as possible, noting the dull smell of staleness, as if the air here hadn't moved for quite a while. A faint mustiness, like leftover hay clippings, permeated the space. Upon that realization, she almost sat straight up, suddenly sure she was inside the barn.

She had so many questions. What had happened? Who had hit her? Where was she? Where was Monte? And probably the most important one—why?

Fighting an overwhelming sense of helplessness, she willed herself not to panic. Although she didn't want to draw attention to herself, she had to know where she was, so she slowly opened her eyes once again. As her vision gradually acclimated to the darkness, she recognized she was staring up at a ceiling. The raw weathered boards were a smoky gray caused by years of unknown upkeep. Her eyes glanced around further, and she realized the thousands of bugs that she'd thought she had seen before were actually hay dust particles circulating through the air.

A faint light was coming from the corner of the room, and she soundlessly turned her head toward the glow. A lantern was hanging from a nail on the barn wall, casting a dark shadow over the individual sitting beside hay bales stacked in the corner. Raelynn couldn't make out much about his appearance. He looked preoccupied and wasn't paying direct attention to her. It seemed he had something in his hands, but she couldn't tell what it was.

Raelyn tried to move again, but the intense pain in her head came back with a vengeance, causing a small groan to escape her mouth. Oh god—he had heard her. When her captor turned his head in her direction, she audibly gasped, unable to believe what she was seeing. She had trusted him, but deep down, she'd known something was off all along.

"Welcome back, Detective Bailey," he said as turned her way. Raelynn gritted her teeth and tried to sit up but was unsuccessful. With a glance, she observed that both of her wrists were secured with zip ties attached to rings inserted into the floor. Despite the restraints keeping her upper body still, she was able to lift her legs and bend her knees, but with every movement, her body ached. Was that promising or ominous?

Her shoes had been removed, and she could feel the coolness of the barn wood under her bare feet. Like living a dream, she imagined Kate in this exact scenario, scrabbling her naked feet against the floor, struggling against zip ties that only became tighter and tighter, cutting into her wrists. Clenching her jaw, Raelynn resisted the urge to react in the same way, knowing it would be futile.

"Why are you doing this?" she asked, more angry than scared in that moment. Her voice was husky, and she felt the urgent need for something to drink. With an unsettling grin, he approached her, then squatted down to get close to her face. In fact, he was so close she thought he was going to kiss her. She could feel his breath on her cheek while she kept her eyes trained on the ceiling.

"You found out my secret," he replied, hovering there for an extra second before moving away. She followed him with her eyes as he circled her, ending at her feet. "I heard you're up for the chief's position. You're a good investigator."

Raelynn ignored his inane chatter. "Is this where you brought Kate?"

"Ah, Kate. Yes, I brought her here." He shook his head in mock disappointment. "You see, Kate had a secret too. I tried to help her, but it was no use. She needed me too much. I had to let her go." He was now pacing, appearing more agitated than he sounded.

"What secret? I don't understand. Were you having an affair with her?" she asked. All of a sudden, the manic look in his eyes dimmed, and he sat back down on the hay bales, putting his head in his hands. In that instant, she actually believed he was remorseful for his decision.

"Affair?" he repeated quietly. "No, I wouldn't call it an affair. I was just trying to help her."

"Help her? She's dead! How did you help her?" As Raelynn spoke, she realized the pain in her head was softening into a dull thump. In fact, she was feeling more and more coherent as the conversation progressed.

"She would have killed herself anyway," he replied, waving his hand dismissively. "I couldn't help her even though I tried. I tried to make her quit, but she just couldn't." He was becoming more excited as he talked about Kate. "I found her one day down by the river. If I hadn't been there, she would have left us that day. She was a user, Raelynn. An addict. She was addicted to heroin."

Raelynn stared at him in disbelief. Kate had had an addiction problem? Sure, Kate had been struggling, and they'd found track marks during the autopsy, but Raelynn assumed it was just a recent thing—nothing serious. "How can that be? She was so put together. She didn't *look* like an addict."

"That's what she wanted everyone to think. But she was messed up. She would have her good days, but most were bad. I sat and watched her. She had all kinds of suppliers who would come into the café. She had no idea I knew." He paused a moment, lost in thought. Then, he continued, shaking his head. "Kate thought I could give her the life she wanted. She took it too far. I couldn't let it go on any longer."

"So you killed her?" Raelynn just wanted to keep him talking. The more he talked, the more time she had to try to figure out how to get out of her situation. She didn't want to be his third victim. As she perpetuated the conversation, she surreptitiously eyed her surroundings, looking for a way out.

"I didn't have any other choice. So I promised her the world. I picked her up after she closed at The Roast. I told her we were going away together, just our little secret. That's when I brought her here."

"Why here? Why the barn?"

"I've known about this place since I got married. I used to come out here to hunt. No one used it, and it was so far away from civilization, I figured no one would figure it out." He paused and looked at Raelynn. "That is, until you did."

Raelynn could see the intense look in his eyes, which appeared almost black. She had never seriously suspected him. What kind of an investigator was she anyway? How could she have missed what was right in front of her all along?

Apparently riled up again, he stood from the bale of hay and began to pace around the confines of the room. Shadows jumped around the space as he passed her, the kerosene lamp giving the effect of several people in the room at once. Raelynn followed his movements, aware she needed to keep an eye on him at all times. While he seemed distracted, she tried to lift her arms but still made no progress in freeing herself. On the bright side, she had feeling in her fingers and was able to pull her hands into fists, trying to get the blood flowing again. Unfortunately, her feet were another story. Although her lower extremities were unrestrained, she couldn't manage to get them working as they should. Her lower body felt numb. She figured it was from lying flat on the floor for God knew how long. Even if she found a way to escape, she wasn't sure she could rely on her body to get her out of there.

"Why Abby then?" Raelynn asked, recapturing his attention.

"I knew Abby's secret too," he responded.

"Which was what? I knew about her background. Was that her secret?" Raelynn's attitude was becoming a bit hostile. She could sense the change in her own demeanor and knew it was risky, but she was running out of time and wanted to hear answers. At the same time, she discreetly lifted her head and was heartened to realize that the movement didn't strike her with dizziness.

Meanwhile, he had walked back to his seat, almost looking ashamed. He held his head with both hands as his elbows rested on his knees. "How'd you find out?" Now he was flipping the questions onto her. Fine, she'd play this game.

"She told me herself. Although I doubt she told me as much as she told you," Raelynn revealed. "You know I went and talked to Nate, right?" Now, she was going to throw the ball into his court—see how much he really did know about Abby.

"I took pity on her. She needed attention, and I gave her that," he began. Raelynn waited, not wanting to interrupt. Since he was sitting again, she was better able to get her bearings around the room, starting with the corner where he was seated. She wanted to see what vulnerabilities were around him. Was he near a door? She *needed* to find a way out.

"She definitely wasn't as pretty as Kate. I would actually say she was a bit plain. I found out quickly that she was naïve, which wasn't too unexpected, especially since she was kept away from reality most of her married life."

Raelynn was listening and scanning the room. Not far from the top of the rafters, she saw an open space. It looked like some type of ventilation area. Having grown up in the country, she knew that a barn had to have ventilation; otherwise, the hay would catch fire. The opening was too small for her to squeeze through, but there had to be another opening the size of a door nearby. Most barns had one or two doors on the main floor and then a loft door above to throw the hay bales through. If she recalled correctly, the main floor of her grandfather's barn was separated into sections. One housed sheep in pens, one was used as a chicken coop, and another had an outdoor space connected for the pigs. Perhaps this barn had a similar layout.

"What did she tell you?" he demanded, clearly wanting to learn more about the victim he hadn't gotten to know well enough before acting on his carnal urges.

Raelynn met his gaze. "That she had to escape. She said that Nate had control of her, but she still loved him on some level," she began. "I wasn't too impressed with him actually. That's just my personal opinion. I could tell that he loved her, but it was definitely a messed-up situation." As she spoke, she saw him nod his head in agreement. "What I don't understand is why you had to kill her?" She decided it was time to broach the subject.

"'Cause she got too close. Abby was influenced by anyone and anything. She was used to being told what to do. She couldn't make choices on her own. How was she to going to set up a new life on her own?" He asked the question and answered it too. "She couldn't. I found the house for her to stay in. I suggested she get the job at The Roast. I made her decisions for her."

The more he talked about Abby, the more aggravated he became. Clearly, he was blaming her for her own death. "She was so needy. I didn't need someone else to take care of. I take care of this whole town!"

Raelynn could tell he was genuinely frustrated just talking about this—to the point that he was getting louder as he went on. Too bad they were out in the middle of nowhere, and no one would be able to hear his rising voice. More agitated than ever, he stood up and started pacing again, and Raelynn knew her window of opportunity was slowly closing. As shadows bounced off the wall behind him, she wracked her brain for a plan—any plan—to escape, but nothing came to mind.

Raelynn hadn't noticed it until now, but he was dressed in everyday clothes and only had his gun on his side. At some point, he had changed out of his uniform. While towering menacingly over her, he constantly swung his arms back and forth. One hand was balled into a fist, and as his arms came together, he would pound his fist into his other palm. The sound of the resulting thuds struck fear into her heart.

Raelynn shut her eyes, accepting that she wasn't going to get out of this mess. He had his own plan set in place, and she had walked right into it. Raelynn was in fight-or-flight mode, but she knew her body would never allow her to take flight. Although she was gradually regaining the ability to move her toes and feet, she was still incapable of running. That only left one option: to fight. But how?

Further feeling out her current predicament, she pulled on the restraints on her arms, but they only grew tighter and tighter, cutting into her skin with each movement. Clearly, she couldn't count on her hands. As she was debating her situation, he stepped closer, then slowly knelt down and placed one knee on each side of her until he was straddling her hips. Now, she was really screwed. Even if she could move, his body weight would pin her to the floor.

With an odd expression distorting his features, he placed one hand on each side of her head and brought his face within inches of hers. Panic beginning to consume her body, Raelynn's vision grew hazy in response to her distress. Her breathing became shallow and quick as a thousand thoughts began swarming her mind.

While looking him directly in the eyes, she caught movement in her peripheral vision behind his back. Her heart leapt with hope, but she didn't dare break eye contact. She wanted him to know she wasn't afraid of him—even though she was internally freaking out. She hoped her mind wasn't playing tricks on her and it wasn't just the lantern casting imaginary shadows throughout the room.

He slowly picked up his hand and ever so gently touched the side of her face. He moved his hand slowly down her cheek, then cupped her throat, pausing slightly before continuing down to her chest. She watched as his gaze followed his hand.

Raelynn used Monte's preoccupation with her body to see what had caught her eye in the corner. The imaginary shadows had silently taken shape. With a flood of relief, she recognized she would be safe. Barely considering the consequences, she took that opportunity to free herself.

Raelynn took a deep breath and closed her eyes. Then, as hard as she could, she lifted her head, aiming straight for his. She made contact with a hard thud and heard the crunch of her nose breaking against his head. The pain was overwhelming, and she could sense herself start to slip away. As the world began to go dark, she felt the weight of his body fall onto her. The rest was a blur.

CHAPTER
39

Raelynn's eyes fluttered open to sunlight streaming through the window. Similar to the last time she'd opened her eyes, it took her a moment to gather her senses, but at least this time, it was due to brightness. Still, she was afraid to move too fast for fear that darkness would overwhelm her again. Luckily, that didn't seem likely, as the white walls reflected the sunlight, and she could see fine dust playing in the rays. The room was warm but sterile with the scent of bleach. It seemed she was safe.

Raelynn looked around the hospital room. She hadn't necessarily been in a room like this since her dad had passed away—other than in her dreams. She took a deep breath in and waited for the flashbacks of that time, but none came. Raelynn's wrists were bandaged, and she had a slight headache, but otherwise, she was relatively unharmed. Most importantly, she was alive.

In the corner of the room, Sergeant Riley sat in an attitude of casual repose. At first, she was unsure who it was, as he was not wearing his standard green uniform. However, she quickly recognized him as she drank in his relaxed form. His head was resting on his bent arm, which was suspended by the arm of the chair. He wore a T-shirt and jeans, and a baseball cap rested on his knee. Unbidden, a smile claimed her face. There was no doubt his shadow had saved her life in that barn. She would be forever grateful.

Raelynn silently watched him until he woke. She didn't know how long he had been there, but she guessed a while. Finally, his eyes fluttered open. After swiping a hand across his face, he stood and walked to her side.

"Hi," he greeted her with a smile. "Welcome back."

"Thanks. How long have I been here?"

"Only a day. You hit him good. I do have to say, though, I wouldn't get any pictures taken anytime soon," he recommended with a sly grin. His remark made Raelynn laugh and, in turn, sent a dagger of pain through her head. As she held her forehead in agony, Sergeant Riley grabbed the visitor chair and brought it over to the bedside.

"How did you figure it out?" she asked as he took his seat.

"I saw the picture at Darla's," he stated simply.

"What picture? I don't understand."

"She had a picture of the old barn on her fireplace mantel."

He paused to gather his thoughts. Raelynn took the opportunity to try to sit up a bit more in the hospital bed. No sooner had she lifted her head than the room started doing 360s around her. She felt Sergeant Riley grab her and place a pillow behind her head, giving her a little leverage.

"I'm okay, at least for now. You can go ahead with your story," she said reassuringly. "I think I know what picture you're talking about. I never thought much about it. I just thought it was a standard print of an ordinary barn. What made you think otherwise?" Raelynn asked.

"I'm not really sure. I just asked, and she told me the barn had been in her family for years. If it was hers, then Monte definitely had access to it," he explained. "The realization on her face when she saw where I was headed was unbelievable. I ran straight out the door and tried to figure out exactly where the barn was."

"Why didn't I put the pieces together?" Although it was a question, she meant it as a statement. "I was so blind! I put myself in that circumstance. I would have died if you hadn't figured it out," she exclaimed, shaking her head sadly.

"Well, I'm glad I did," he said as he gently took her hand in his. Raelynn let her gaze travel from their hands to his eyes. She smiled in response, but even that hurt. "You're going to be okay, and that's all that matters."

"I can't thank you enough," she stated effusively. She could feel a tear run down her cheek.

"We have the rest of our lives for you to thank me," he quipped with a suggestive wink. Then, with supreme tenderness and care, he raised her hand and placed a light kiss to the top.

It had taken two murders and the near sacrifice of her own life, but she had finally found the glimmer of happiness she had never even realized she'd been seeking all along. And in that moment, Raelynn knew her life had changed for good.